EVIL ON THE PEACE RIVER

By Beverly Lein

INKWATER PRESS

PORTLAND • OREGON
INKWATERPRESS.COM

Scan this QR Code
to learn more about
this title

Publisher: Inkwater Press | www.inkwaterpress.com

Paperback
ISBN-13 978-1-59299-758-9 | ISBN-10 1-59299-758-9

Kindle
ISBN-13 978-1-59299-759-6 | ISBN-10 1-59299-759-7

Printed in the U.S.A.
All paper is acid free and meets all ANSI standards for archival quality paper.

1 3 5 7 9 10 8 6 4 2

Evil on the Peace River

DEDICATION

I would like to dedicate this book to my late parents, Mary and William Ressler. I truly wish that my dad would have lived to see my books but he never did.

My dad loved reading and dreams and thought that nothing was impossible to do if you wanted to do something bad enough.

My mother was scared of everything and we were thankful for Dad who always played the balancing act.

But to Mom's credit she taught us to work, to be honest and stick to anything we started, and it must have been a bit hard on her raising the seventh child, Dad.

I would like to thank Dianne Smyth, my editor, whose support is never failing.

I would like to thank Rachel, my publicist, and her sister Kyla who slowed me down, took the book, and ironed out some factors that needed redoing. Thank you both so much. You're a pair of little life saviours.

Of course, last but not least, to my grandchildren Brittany, Morgan, Sydnee, Rachel and Ashley, who are patiently waiting for Grandma's book to come out.

What an amazing support group.

Love you all.

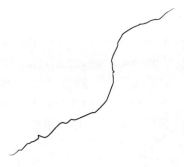

Sheets of rain bounced off the ground as Jack Nickels watched through the panelled glass doors. He rubbed the back of his neck, feeling uneasy for some reason. He had never felt this way in all the years he had been a security guard at the Peace River Correctional Centre. He just couldn't shake the uncomfortable feeling that he was being watched.

"Impossible," he muttered. "It's just me and Bill. Bill checked the cells and everyone's accounted for."

But as he turned away from the door, he missed the slow but stealthily moving shadow of someone creeping toward the side of the building. Despite the brilliant outside lights it was hard to see anything through the driving rain of that the dark night.

Reassured, Jack sauntered back to his desk and flopped down to the nightly sign-in sheets. "I must be nuts...everything's fine."

"Might as well get going on this stuff," he mumbled to himself as he reached for a stack of papers. He had barely picked up his pen when he heard something hard hit the glass door. It sounded like a rock. He jumped up, glancing at his watch, and looked down the long hallway for Bill. He moved toward the door, imagining the he was hearing the sounds of someone who wanted in out of the rain.

"Funny, why didn't they just push the buzzer?"

Even wiping the condensation off the door didn't help—he couldn't see a thing. He was sure no one was there, but the sound of whatever had struck the door was still sharp in his mind. So he pulled down his cap and stepped out into the rain, leaving the door open behind him. Nothing.

Must have been the rain hitting the glass, he thought. *Maybe hail.*

Stepping back into the warmth of the entrance, he saw small puddles on the floor in front of him. By the time it dawned on him that he could not have left those puddles himself, something hit him hard from behind. The dripping-wet man with the baseball bat made his way behind the desk, pulling the lifeless body of Jack Nickels with him.

Simon looked down at the body and grinned sadistically. Excitement coursed through him. Killing always gave him satisfaction and the rush followed was euphoric. He quickly removed the security guard's revolver and tucked it into his belt. If he was going to free Kip, it was now or never.

Sliding the guard's keys off his belt he ran down the hallway leading to the cells and searched for No. 8. He made his way cautiously down the corridor and reaching his brother's cell quickly unlocked the door and slid it open. Kip quickly crept out of the dark room and joined his brother.

Simon and Kip had picked tonight for the escape because the prison was always shorthanded on Thursdays. The storm was an unexpected plus. As the heavy thunder shook the prison walls, lightning ripped across the sky and the heavy darkness left in its wake made it impossible to see. The brothers glued themselves to the wall and moved carefully down the hallway as they approached the glass-panelled security office that lay at the end of the cell block.

Still holding the baseball bat, Simon approached the office where Bill Sanders sat reading and knocked quietly. Hearing what he thought was his colleague, Jack, at the door, Bill rose to open the door laughing at what he assumed was his friend's foolishness in forgetting his office key yet again. As he opened the door his laughter died his throat.

It wasn't Jack standing before him. It was the new guard, Guy Ladour; Guy wasn't supposed to be on duty tonight. That brief moment was all it took for Guy to raise the bat high above his head and before Bill had time to reach for his revolver the bat had struck with deadly force.

Simon smirked. It sure had paid off, taking that job as a security guard for the last month. He knew his way around the prison like the back of his hand, and better than that – he knew their routines and habits. It had been easy enough to get in the door with an assumed identity. Just like that Simon Drosset of Sault Ste Marie had become 'Guy Ladour': upstanding Ontario citizen. And Ladour's clean as the pure driven snow background and virtually guaranteed him the job.

Simon had met Guy Ladour at a bar. The man was tipsy and in the mood to talk. What attracted Simon to the stranger was the uncanny likeness they shared—they could have passed for twins. Of course, the stranger was just as amused as Simon was at this coincidence. With liquid lubrication, Guy told Simon his life's story, that he was an only child and that he'd been looking after his elderly mother. That he'd recently moved her into a nursing home because of her dementia. And he also told Simon his mother had plenty of money. Guy had set up a local trust with her attorneys freeing him up from the burden of even having to write cheques for her care. Simon listened, intrigued. It couldn't have been more perfect.

The man continued to brag about his good fortune, saying he didn't have to work because his mother's wealth had ensured he was well-heeled but out of pride he still worked as a security guard.

"Yup, got all my papers, all my references – I can pretty much work anywhere!" he'd told Simon.

Simon's mind went into overdrive, trying to figure out how to get this man to leave the bar with him and set a plan of action into motion. It was easier than he could have hoped.

As the night wore on, Guy mentioned his growing hunger to his new friend – an opportunity Simon pounced on.

"Listen, what say you give me a ride home and I'll cook you up a bite at my place?"

Guy, believing he had found a kindred spirit quickly accepted, "Sounds good. I'm starving. Haven't eaten since lunch. Came here for a quick beer at three and look how late it is already. Lord knows I've had enough to drink, that's for sure." Guy stood up from his bar stool and Simon steadied his staggering body.

"Sorry 'bout that," Guy said. "Guess I had more than enough. How 'bout you drive?" Guy asked, handing Simon the keys.

As they walked toward the door Simon caught his reflection in the window. He was tall and neatly dressed with dark brown hair and eyes. He couldn't believe his luck finding a man who bore such an uncanny physical resemblance to himself. But the physical resemblance is where the similarities ended.

There was no warmth to Simon Drosset. He was cruel, cold, and calculating he was a man without a conscience. He made his way through life stealing, forging, lying, and if need be, killing. The thought of getting a job and 'earning' a living never even crossed his mind. Not that he couldn't have—he was as sharp as a whip and had made good grades in school. But Simon knew there was something missing in his makeup that would allow him to fit in with the regular working world.

The only person he had any feeling for—or at least a sense of duty to protect—was his younger brother Kip. At home he had protected him from their abusive mother and their drunken father, at school he had shielded him from bullies, and on the street he'd kept him out of the target of gangs. It often irritated Simon that his brother didn't seem to have any brains and usually got caught robbing people or pushing drugs, which was how he'd ended up in the clink in Peace River, Alberta. How exactly he had ended up out west Simon didn't know, but he was doing five years for rape, and kidnapping, and armed robbery with violence.

The last letter Simon had received worried him. Kip sounded depressed and desperate; he talked of killing himself. Simon shrugged his shoulders, trying to get the kid off his mind. How many times Simon had confined and raped women himself he couldn't even count—but he'd never been caught. Sometimes he'd hang around a crime scene just for laughs watching the cops prod and question witnesses. He had to laugh, because it always seemed like every witness gave a different description of him. Once when he was being questioned, he described himself pretty accurately to an officer just to see his reaction. The officer didn't bat an eye, just took down his description, thanked him, and went on to question someone else. He'd had a good laugh over that one. Even just to think of it brought a nasty grin to his face.

As Simon helped Guy into the passenger side of the car he laughed at the idiocy of this jerk who had just handed over his keys to a complete stranger. If he'd only known what was in store for him he'd have jumped out of the car right then and there. But Simon figured that if a 40-year-old man didn't know better, then he deserved whatever he had coming. It was the same way he justified what happened to the various women who got into his car. If a woman was stupid enough to go along with him willingly and she ended up beaten or dead, well it was her fault for going with him willingly—she shouldn't have trusted him.

As they drove up to Simon's rented room, he parked at the back of the motel. The fewer people who saw him with anyone, the safer he'd be. Once inside, Guy made himself comfortable, removing his coat and loosening his tie. He fell into the easy chair, "Boy, this feels good."

"Yeah, it does," said Simon, with a smirk. "I'll put the coffee on and bring you a cup soon as it's ready." As Simon measured the coffee into the pot, Guy asked him what he did for a living. The motel room looked cheap; Guy didn't think the man had much money. Yet, his clothes shoes looked expensive.

Simon replied, "I'm into banking, I'm always looking for ways to make easy money."

Guy nodded, "Well, if you ever find one, let me know!"

"Scrambled eggs and toast good enough?"

"You bet," Guy said. "I could eat a horse." Simon poured two cups of coffee slipping some of the knockout drops he carried into one. For special suckers like Guy, he'd always preferred this home remedy. Handing the coffee to Guy, he switched on the TV and saying cheerfully, "There, you can catch the news while I finish cooking."

When the eggs and toast were done he filled a single plate with food and raised his cup to salute the man now sleeping in the chair.

"Sweet dreams buddy."

After he enjoyed a leisurely meal Simon he walked over to the drugged man and pulled the wallet from the inside pocket of his jacket. Counting bills, Simon was ecstatic to find $500 in twenties and a few small bills. Next, he found his bank book, chequebook, his birth certificate, his social insurance number, and his driver's license. It was an excellent haul. After looking through his car Simon hit the final jackpot: Guy's work papers.

It really did seem to him like luck just had a way of following him through his life. Nobody could stop him now! As he flipped through the papers he got a thrill at seeing just how much the photo on the driver's license looked like a reflection of him.

Beside him, the sleeping body's breath was growing increasingly laboured. It wouldn't be long before he breathed his last breath. Simon had given Guy more than enough of the drug to kill him. After all, it was better than shooting or knifing. They were too messy and he'd have enough mess to clean up after the last jobs he had to do.

Finally, Guy had exhaled his last painful breath. Pulling a hacksaw and pliers out of his toolbox, Simon began the gruesome job of erasing the dying man's physical identity. One by one, he pried the teeth from the dead man's mouth—immune to the crunching sounds that came from prying bone from gum. Then he slowly and methodically severed each digit from the corpse's hands, gleefully ripping through the remaining tendons and muscles after having hacked through the bone.

His work done, he picked up the body and rolled it back up onto the couch. Taking his own wallet out of his pocket, Simon threw it into the couch where it waited to be found alongside the body. He packed an overnight bag with the bare essentials, making sure not to take too much. He walked to the doorway, tossing a match behind him and closed the door on a smouldering flame; he'd be well away before the fire had overtaken the room. And with that, he walked out the door leaving behind Simon Drosset; he was a new man now, he was Guy Ladour.

Jane Hall tucked the last hair in place and picked up the hairspray. Just as she started to apply it, she heard something on the radio about a shooting. Putting down the can, she hurried over and turned up the radio. The broadcast was out of Peace River, about 65 miles southeast of Manning, where the announcer said there had also been a shooting. She listened closely to hear of news of people she knew in her hometown, but the announcement was sketchy and police would of course have to notify the family first.

Jane, a thirty-year-old who had lived on her own for a long time, was attractive, with short dark-brown hair and deep brown eyes. Of medium height, she kept in shape by leading an active lifestyle and through daily horseback riding. She lived in the hills of the Peace River in a small cottage-style home about 20 miles east of Manning. It wasn't too big but it suited her needs. The little house sat on a quarter section of land, land that she rented to a farmer. She had bought the property for the house and its barn.

Jane's live-in companion was her dog Sam, a big golden collie who was deeply devoted to her. In the corral were her two horses, Misty and Charlie. Misty, a gentle-natured seven-year-old mare had incredible stamina and liked being the packhorse. Charlie was a high-spirited gelded mustang. Jane had been working with him a lot and he was really coming around, but he still figured he was the boss. He had been a stud for too long before he was gelded and his urge to mate was still strong.

As she tidied the house and made breakfast Jane kept the radio on, hoping to hear news of who might have been hurt. Five minutes later, the news broke in on the radio announcing a prison break from the Peace River Correctional Centre. The RCMP thought the shooting and the prison break might be related and they warned listeners that if approached by any strange men that they were to be regarded as potentially armed and dangerous. The news update gave no additional details about the shooting.

Jane had made plans to go on a horseback camping trip through the Peace River hills. She intended to start from Weasel's Flat, a valley nestled near the Peace River, and travel to the town of Peace River. She planned on being on her own for about a month. Weasel's Flat was on the west side of the region, deep in the hills. Cabins sat on the banks overlooking the Peace and it was a gorgeous place in the summer where many of her friends gathered for boating, waterskiing, and hiking. They spent their winters there skiing and tobogganing with evening hot chocolates and drinks in front of a bonfire to keep warm.

From Weasel's Flat she would then go on to Sunny Valley, another vast area where the Peace River flowed through. She planned to stop there to visit with neighbours before leaving for the Cadott, on the east side of the river. The Cadott was a super fishing spot but since she would be starting off on the west side she'd have to see if there were any boats available for her to cross to the other side. Her next stop would be the White and then further downriver, Tar Island, a tourist attraction with rental cabins. Her final destination was the town of Peace River.

Peace River was, give or take, 75 to 85 miles away. Travelling the hills up and down the canyon she'd be lucky to make four or five miles a day. If she could follow the river she'd make better time, but whenever she had to climb the hills it would be slow going.

The radio snapped Jane back to reality as the announcer finally broadcast the tragic details of the shooting. Jane listened to the details, unnerved by the fact that the escaped prisoner and the man who had helped him break out had killed two security guards and had made their to the outskirts of Manning to a farmyard just out of town. Under the ruse that they had run out of gas, they had forced their way into the home of a young couple, Taylor and Kim Doyle, where they demanded money, guns, and food. They'd shot the husband and attacked the wife, leaving her for dead, before grabbing the couple's four-year-old son, Devon on their way out.

Jane was horrified. She was good friends with both the Doyles and the Chansons. She quickly phoned their mutual neighbour Agnes Smith who told Jane everything she knew. Apparently Jim Chanson, Kim's father, had stopped in to drop off some tools he had picked up in Grimshaw for his son-in-law. Seeing the lights on, he decided to stop in and let them know he'd left them out in the garage. As he walked up to the house, he noticed the door wasn't closed. He called out, but nobody answered. So he went into the house to discover his daughter in the bedroom, beaten almost beyond recognition. In the living room he found Taylor tied up and slumped over. Apparently Kim managed to give police a description before losing consciousness. Her husband was in critical condition and the whereabouts of Devon, their son, were unknown.

At the hospital, two Manning doctors were fighting to save Taylor Doyle's life. They'd been able to remove the bullet, but he had lost an incredible amount of blood. Kim too had sustained life-threatening injuries with most of the bones in her face and skull shattered. They had both made it out of surgery, but their conditions were still critical.

Jane's phone rang steadily all morning as news of the Doyle family tragedy spread through the small town and surrounding farming community. She wondered if she should delay her trip for a few days until the killers had been apprehended. But according to the police report, the killers were heading either north to the Territories or south to Edmonton.

The following day Agnes called back to tell her that Taylor now had a good chance of recovery, but that Kim was still drifting in and out of consciousness. Before any surgeries to attempt to repair the damage to her face could be undertaken, the doctors had to stop the swelling in her brain. Jane thanked her friend for phoning and told her she would get in touch with the families in the evening to offer her support. She desperately hoped Kim survived. She was such a lovely young woman; she loved her husband and son unconditionally. Jane bowed her head and said a quick prayer that Kim would survive and that the child would be found alive.

That evening when Jane phoned the Chansons, Jim answered. His wife Dee was in the city at her daughter's bedside and Jim had stayed behind to help search for Devon. Crying, he thanked Jane for phoning and told her that the doctor's seemed to be having some success reducing the swelling in Kim's brain.

"Thank God," Jane whispered. "Jim, I feel so helpless. I'd like to help. Is there anything you need?"

Jim said, "I'm out of bread."

Jane had to laugh, "I'll bring some over to you. I'm packing to leave on my riding excursion and I've got bread to give away."

Her packing done, Jane drove the 15 miles to the Chanson's farm and delivered the bread.

"Shucks, Janie," Jim said, "you didn't have to do this. It's only four miles to town. I could have run in and got some."

"It's okay, I wanted to come anyway. You got coffee on?"

"Yes, I've got cakes, cookies, squares, any goodies you can name. The community ladies are looking after me real good, but nobody brought any sandwiches or bread."

Jane stayed an hour, consoling her friend. As she prepared to head out she said, "Tell Dee I'm praying for her. I know these things are hell on parents, especially mothers."

"Yeah," Jim said. "But you know if I got my hands on those two bastards for one second I'd kill them with my bare hands!"

Jim said, "When do you leave?"

"Tomorrow. I want to get an early start but if I don't that's okay."

Hugging her dear friend goodbye, she said, "For the life of me, I'll never understand the evil that people can do to others."

Jane's friends were all aware of her impending trail ride, but some were a little worried about her. She'd done the trail ride at least seven times before with her father and friends, but this would be her first time alone. The understanding was that if she didn't show up in Peace River by the end of the month, they were to contact the RCMP. She'd be lying if she didn't admit that the recent events had made her a little more nervous about the trip. But despite the drizzle and brewing storm clouds Jane awoke to in the morning, she felt good about her plans.

Misty nickered as Jane approached the corral. A good-natured animal, Misty made an ideal packhorse. It always took a little time to unpack or repack a horse, so she placed things in separate bags and marked what was in each. She had a small pup tent for herself and Sam. Although she planned to hunt and fish for fresh meat, she also stocked up with cans of meat, vegetables, and fruit. Jane was sure of her strength and her ability with a rifle, and she wasn't squeamish about shooting or skinning an animal. After all, she had done it with her father all her life.

A lump formed in her throat as she thought of her dad who'd had a sudden heart attack a year ago. With no past illnesses and her father being in such good shape, it had been a terrible shock to her. Her mother had died when she was a child, but she had never felt like she was alone in the world with all her extended family. In fact, one of her uncles had planned to make this trip with her, but some old army buddies had shown up unannounced and taken him along on a holiday to Alaska. It was an opportunity Jane could hardly let him skip out on, and she'd given him her blessing to go.

It was 11 o'clock by the time Jane headed down the hill to the river's edge, heading towards Weasel's Park. The river was low this year so she could do a lot of riding right down by the water's edge. She could easily cover the 10 or so miles to Sunny Valley, where she planned to spend the night and visit her friends, Marcy and Wayne. Marcy thought Jane was out of her mind—she couldn't comprehend of someone even wanting to ride the Peace River hills on horseback, let alone cover the 90-mile trip up and down the deep canyons. Jane tried to explain how exhilarating and challenging it was, but her friend had always just shaken her head in disbelief.

The drizzling rain didn't slow the horses down. For them, the rain was a wonderful reprieve from bull flies and other biting insects. As Jane rode along her thoughts remained focused on her father. He had so loved their trail rides through the Peace River hills. Laughing to herself she wondered if she would run into Baldie. He would be five years old now if he was still alive.

Years ago she and her father had come across a dead sow with a cub still trying to nurse on her. By the look of the situation the mother had tried to protect her cub from a male bear and had been killed in the process. The cinnamon-coloured cub had probably been attacked by the male first; he was missing his ear and his head had been badly chewed. He had been so hungry and dehydrated when they found him that he'd come right up to them to see if they were a source for food. Her dad had quickly opened a couple of cans of canned milk and the cub devoured them greedily.

Jane had so fallen in love with the bear that she'd ended up caring for him under the guidance of local rangers. Giving the cub just enough contact to be nurtured but no so much that he would become human-dependent upon his eventual release, Jane had built a fence on their acreage where he could roam and grow. They'd named him Baldie as the hair on the part of his head where he'd been bitten had never grown back. Finally, when Baldie had reached age three the rangers had advised Jane it was time to release the bear back into the wild.

After a tearful and emotional parting the rangers had taken in a cage and turned him loose in bear territory. Understandably Jane had been worried about him, but over the months her worry lessened – she'd always had a good feeling about that little guy.

Now, as she rode on her in her solitary quest, her eyes feasted on the wonder and beauty of the hills and thoughts of Baldie fled her mind. They reached Sunny Valley at about seven o'clock without mishap, not having sighted any large game. It seemed odd not to see moose, bear, or deer by the river, but what was stranger was not having seen even a beaver or a coyote.

At the house Marcy had supper waiting. After Wayne
helped Jane stable the horses in the big barn, the three of
them had supper on the veranda and shared a few drinks.
Watching the drizzling rain fill the puddles in the yard until
they were overflowing, Marcy said, "I wish we were kids
again."

"Remember? We used to follow the water until it got
to the big culvert." With no place else to go, the water was
making its way to the ditch.

"Yeah," Jane said. "Then we got a smacking from our
mothers for playing near the culvert. What if we'd gotten
sucked into one? We would have drowned. If I remember
correctly that was *your* idea!"

Marcy laughed, "Yeah, I came up with lots of crazy
schemes, didn't I?" As the evening wore on, the conversa-
tion turned to the tragedy in Peace River and the Doyle
family. Marcy and Wayne, who had a four-year-old son, were
deeply concerned about the little boy.

Marcy said, "I hope they find the little guy alive. Why
take him? Why would anybody take a little child?"

They went to bed that night their hearts heavy from
worry about the ailing parents and the missing boy's future.

In Ottawa, Cam Jensen, a thirty-eight-year-old seasoned
homicide police officer was working on the death of a Simon
Drosset. He had been given the case three months ago when
the body, missing its teeth and fingers, had been sent to their
office. Cam kept coming up dry on the investigation with no
leads, no witnesses and one hell of a burnt-up corpse. But
one thing was for sure: anyone who'd had anything to do
with the Simon Drosset hadn't liked him one bit.

Cam had learned that the man was vicious, that no one
trusted him, and that everyone felt that he was hiding things

from the rest of the world—bad things. Finally, after four months Cam had gotten a break. He'd managed to connect with someone who knew a Simon Drosset who had travelled to St. Joseph Island, not far from the city. The man said that Drosset sometimes visited Hilton Beach on Lake Huron, a popular boating destination for seasonal residents and tourists. Of the 200 permanent residents there, one was named Drosset.

Cam pulled up in front of the modest old-style cottage, yawned and stretched, and stepped out of his car. He was a powerfully built man with steel blue eyes that could look right through you. He often appeared unapproachable, that is, until he smiled. With sandy blonde hair and a strong square chin, he was well over six feet tall in his stocking feet. The cleft in his chin gave him a stern look but the dimple in his right cheek when he smiled made the ladies' hearts flutter. He'd never met a woman he wanted to marry. Not that he ever had time for a relationship, being a homicide detective who travelled a lot. He never knew where the next lead would take him or what town he would wake up in, and that didn't work well for relationships. In the end, Cam was a man's man, and his co-workers admired him and his reliability made him a top choice to partner with on cases.

Cam walked up to the Drosset door and knocked. Perspiration washed down the back of his neck from the hot sun and he used the palm of his hand to dry his forehead. A matronly woman opened the door wiping the flour on her hands off onto a tea towel.

"Hi," she said, "can I help you with something?"

Cam flashed his badge and informed her he was the one who had previously phoned about Simon Drosset.

"Yes, yes!" she exclaimed. "Come in, come right in. I'm Angie Drosset. I was married to Simon's first cousin, Harmon."

"Could you tell me a little about him?" Cam asked as he slipped off his jacket. "Who his friends were, if he was ever married, or had any children?"

Angie looked at him, a frown running across her kind face. "Has something happened to him?"

"Yes," Cam said. "About four months ago we found a body in a motel room rented to a Simon Drosset. We've been trying to find his next of kin ever since." Angie's sharp intake of breath didn't stop surprised him, but he continued, "It was a homicide, and lot of identification markers were missing and the body was badly burnt. The medical examiners are still piecing the evidence together."

"Sit down and I'll make some coffee," Angie ushered Cam into the kitchen. "So life finally caught up with him, huh? Well...as far as I'm concerned, murder still sounds like it was too easy an out for him. He made life rotten for anyone who ever had anything to do with him. What an evil, miserable man."

"What do you mean?" Cam asked, flipping open his notepad. The kitchen fell silent as Angie dried her hands after rinsing off the flour. Cam sensed she was thinking about how to answer the question.

Putting two coffee cups on the table, she shook her head and said, "Simon was just plain bad. Plain bad. I remember when we were kids...Jim, my husband's younger brother, got a bike for his birthday. We all thought it was grand, probably the grandest and most beautiful bike we had ever seen. Well somehow it just disappeared. We kids searched the neigh-bourhood for that bike and we never found it. About two months later the shed at Simon's house was left open and for some reason we looked inside and sure enough we found that bike. It'd been sawed up, smashed, totally mangled, and hidden behind a sheet of plywood. Jim got his dad and they went back to the shed. It was obvious Simon had taken the bike, and his father beat the hell out of him for it. But that didn't stop Simon. He was so angry Jim ratted on him. A few days later Harmon and Jim's dog disappeared, we found it later—the body had been stabbed over and over again and its eyes had been gouged out."

"And you figure it was Simon?" Cam asked with disbe-lief.

"Yeah, couldn't have been nobody else. And that's not all. Their female cat and her kittens disappeared too and later someone found them drowned in a sack. The boys were scared of Simon, but nobody could ever pin anything on him. We just couldn't catch him in the act. Way too sneaky. He used to threaten us too. Like…he'd say if we wouldn't do something his way we'd end up like the bike or the cats or the dog. I was real afraid of him."

Angie paused, and took a deep breath before continuing, "Then…guess I was about 14 or so, and Simon was probably 17, maybe pushing 18. Jim told me he'd found a robin's nest with eggs. He said I had to see them because the eggs were so blue. He told me where the nest was, down close to the lake on an old piece of farm equipment. I went down to see them and just when I was looking in the nest, Simon appears out of nowhere. I think he was following me. I asked him what he was doing there. He didn't say anything. He just reached into the nest. And, one by one, never taking his eyes off me, he crushed those eggs. I screamed at him to stop and tried to hit him. He grabbed me as quick as you please, and threw me to the ground...and he started ripping off my clothes and slapping me. I knew it was gonna get bad, so I screamed as loud as I could. He started choking me and I fought real hard but he was too strong. I thought I was gonna die, and worse. That's when Harmon and Jim showed up with old Mr. Kenny, who beat the hell out of Simon. Then on I made sure I was never alone as long as Simon was around."

"Did they call the police?" asked Cam.

"No, nothin' ever come of it. My dad figured the beating he got from Mr. Kenny was enough. We shoulda, but we didn't."

"Too bad," said the officer, "might have made a difference."

"Yeah, who knows?" Angie shrugged. "From then on, I always stayed as far away from Simon as I could—even after Harmon and me got married."

Angie's voice dropped, "And what's worse is...about a month after the robin's nest thing, Mr. Kenny was found dead at the bottom of a cliff – everyone said it was an accident. But I don't care what anybody says. I know Simon did it. Mr. Kenny walked them hills for years and he sure as hell knew where the edges were. Simon always held a grudge against people that got him mad, big time. I could go on and on with things he done. He was one cruel and mean SOB. The only one he was half decent to was his younger brother, Kip. Kip got around Simon 'cause he always did whatever he wanted."

"Tell me about Kip," said the officer, looking up from his notepad.

"Kip? He was bad too, real bad. I think Simon brain-washed him good. Their mom was real abusive and their father was nothin' but a drunk. He beat them whenever he felt like it. Maybe the boys didn't stand much of a chance to be any different. Those two boys never worked—they just swiped whatever they could lay their dirty little hands on. If a girl wouldn't give them the time of day, a few weeks later you would hear that somethin' real bad would've happened to her. The never could prove anything, but us kids? *We* knew who was behind for all the hell in the neighbourhood." Flushed with the emotions from those memories, Angie fell silent, her hand trembling so much that she didn't dare pick up her cup.

Cam finished his coffee, "Sounds like you may be right, the world probably is better off without him." he said.

Pulling a picture from an envelope handing it to Angie he went on, "And we just want to confirm with you that this photo from his driver's license is actually him—can you do that?"

"It's him alright," Angie said after looking carefully at the picture.

"And one other thing," Cam added, "can you confirm that he had a birthmark on his right wrist? It was one of the few things we could make out on his body."

Angie looked puzzled and shook her head, "Simon never had no birthmark on his right wrist. Didn't have no birth-mark at all."

A sense of dread flooded over Cam. Talking as much to the coffee cup as to Angie, he muttered, "Then ... who the hell is this dead guy? And where's Simon Drosset?"

Simon threw more wood into the stove. He and Kip had managed to give the cops the slip and had been travelling cautiously around the back roads. The radio broadcasters had speculated they'd been heading north or south in their warnings to the public when in fact they'd been right in the cops' own backyard. On their way back to Peace River, they'd seen a sign for White Mud and took the turn. They followed the road, ending up down by the river where they'd found some cabins scattered along the banks. With the continuous downpour of rain keeping campers away, the cabins lay empty and breaking in was easy. One of the cabins had a full stock of canned food and they knew they could easily hole up there for a couple of weeks until the heat was off.

Looking across the room, Simon's pitiless eyes settled on the little boy who had cried himself to sleep. He'd planned to toss him in the river before they left. He'd only grabbed the kid as collateral in case they'd been stopped, but now that he was no use to them he'd have to get rid of him soon. His thoughts went back to the boy's parents and he couldn't help but get angry at himself for not putting bullets between both their eyes. He should've been more careful to make sure they were both dead. The last broadcast they'd heard on their transistor radio made it sound like they might survive. "Not good, Simon," he scolded himself, "Never leave witnesses."

Devon woke up and looked over at the man in the chair. He was terrified of that man. He winced as he tried to move the arm he'd hurt when the man had thrown him against the wall. He couldn't think of anything except how much he wanted his parents to come and get him. His stomach growled from lack of food, and fear kept him from even asking for a drink or for permission to go to the bathroom in case it earned him another beating. Sometimes he just peed in his pants rather than ask to go out.

The times when the men drank until they passed out were a relief to Devon; when they were sleeping, they weren't yelling at him. This night, as soon as snores filled the cabin Devon crept off the bed, pulling a blanket with him. Moving silently to the cupboard, he took out a package of crackers and holding them closely, moved towards the door, carefully opened it a crack and looked out into the dark. He was afraid of the dark but he was more afraid of the two men. Inching the door open wider, he stepped quietly out into the dark. The barefoot child, still in the pyjamas he'd been wearing the night of the attack, headed for the heavy bush. Somehow, he knew he had to get as far away from the bad men as he could.

Jane left her friends' house at the crack of dawn. She had to get an early start if she was to make it at least halfway to the Cadott by nightfall. The Cadott was about 40 miles from the valley. Sam spent the day scooting ahead of them and dashing back to greet her and the horses. He'd managed to save her the work of hunting today by catching two prairie chickens and bringing them back to her one by one. With each delivery from Sam Jane swung down from Charlie's back and packed the lifeless chickens into her pack. She'd be sure to reward Sam for his hard work once it'd been cooked over a campfire.

They made good time and travelled at least 21 miles in the day by following the trail near the edge of the river and avoiding hills. But the travel was exhausting, so as soon as supper was done and cleaned up, they bedded down. Up early in the next morning, she didn't eat or bother with a fire, despite the chill. The last few days had been overcast with a few showers but this morning the sun, complemented by a scattering of clouds and blue sky, crept over the hills into the valley. It was going to be a beautiful day for a change. Jane hoped the stormy weather was gone for good, especially as there was no way to avoid climbing the hills with the horses now that the river's edge was no longer passable. The day was tough as they traversed up and down the canyons, but soon the cliffs morphed back into being just hills and they could follow the river's edge again. In some places the river was so low that the bigger islands all but reached the shore. She couldn't remember the river ever being so low.

They had almost reached the Cadott and she was hoping she could find a place to camp right on the river's edge. Maybe a boat would go by or maybe there'd be people fishing on the creek. Where the Cadott ran into the Peace, there was a great place for jackfish. It would be nice if she ran into someone she knew, to have some human company. It also would mean she could send word back to her friends about where she was. They were about half a mile from the Cadott when she heard Sam's anxious barking. He had disappeared into the heavy bush and as just she turned the horse toward the barking, Charlie began acting up as well.

"Smarten up boy," Jane growled. "You be good." But Charlie wouldn't calm down and gave a couple of unexpected bucks, unseating her.

"Damn you, Charlie! That hurt!" Jane said picking herself up and rubbing her backside. "Okay, you guys stay here and I'll go see what's going on." She looped the reins over a branch and plucked the rifle out of its scabbard and crept ahead.

She was glad she hadn't forced the horses ahead for there on the ground, securely held by a leg snare, was a large bear. As she walked closer, she stopped and gasped in shock. The bear lying listlessly had no right ear and a very bald spot. "Good Lord Baldie, how did you ever get yourself in this mess?"

Jane worried though, it wasn't normal for the animal to just lie there and not fight to escape—he had to have been trapped there for a long time. A bear could last a long time without food, but she didn't know how long a bear could go without water.

Jane wrestled with what to do next: should she try to help him or just shoot him? With all the rain he wouldn't have been in the hot sun for too long, but she didn't think there was much she could to save them. But before she could raise her rifle the bear let out a weak, pained cry. She set aside the rifle, quietened Sam, and went back to the horses. Untying them, she swung up on Charlie, and headed down-hill to the river where she tethered the horses on long rope, letting them graze and have their fill of water.

Unloading her pack, she filled her billy tin with water and opened a can of sardines. Rummaging through the pack, she cussed under her breath, "Where the hell are my side cutters?" After finding them, she shoved them into her back pocket, took Sam and the rifle, and went uphill with the water and sardines. Jane approached the bear carefully; she had no way of knowing of Baldie would recognize her anymore. Jane crept over to the tree where the snare was tied. Cutting the wire, she then moved closer to the bear's snared leg. Her body tensed and ready to spring back, she looked at the bear's paw. The wire had all but disappeared into the animal's flesh, likely cutting off the circulation. Every time the bear had fought the snare, the snare had automatically tightened further. Cutting through the wire around the tree was easy, but getting at the wire embedded in the bear's leg was far more difficult. Sweating, Jane squeezed the wire cutters as hard as she could until finally the wire snapped and the leg fell free. "You are one lucky bear, and I'm one lucky woman," Jane said, well aware that normally it would take a sedation dart to get this close to a healthy four or five-hundred-pound animal.

Getting up slowly, and keeping the rifle close at hand, she gingerly approached Baldie's head with the tin of water. Jane made sure the path behind her was clear in case she had to jump make a run for it suddenly. But as Jane squatted down the bear remained still and she squatted down next to him. She lifted his big head with one hand and gently trickling water into his mouth with the other. The bear feebly moved his tongue, trying to lap in the water.

At least he wants to live. Jane's nerves tightened like a drum. Setting the sardines down in front of his face, she went back to her riverside camp. After building a fire, she settled down and waited, listening to the distant coyotes and timber wolves howling in the night. She was amazed that predators hadn't killed the bear. Maybe they'd been waiting for it to die. Jane soon fell asleep, the rifle at her side as Sam kept watch throughout the night. The horses whinnied and snorted their discontent knowing that something dangerous lay just up the hill.

Jane slept lightly, waking often to feed the fire. By the time morning came the horses had quietened and Jane made a quick cold, breakfast. She had decided to stall her trip for a while to see how the bear made out. Taking an extra long rope with her and the billy tin of water, she returned to the bear. It had not moved from where she'd left him the night before. She put down the water, alert and tensed for any response from the big animal. But there was nothing, not even when the collie walked cautiously around him, tail tucked securely between his legs. Jane spoke soothingly to the bear while tying his back leg to the tree in case a surge of energy prompted him to attack. Again, she helped the bear drink but this time seemed a little more alert, successfully lapping in more of the water. Jane noticed two sardines missing and hoped it was a positive sign.

Jane rose and looked down at the helpless creature. Five years old," she said. "Prime of life, and this happens! I'm just going down the hill, so you get better now."

Jane fished for the rest of the day; the horses were happy for the break and lay contentedly in the shade. Jane was happy to stay camped here for a while and take it easy as she was still throbbing from Charlie's throw the day before.

That evening Jane and Sam returned to the bear with several fish and a tin bowl of water. The bear seemed stronger and half moved his head as she approached. "Hey, you ate all the sardines!" she exclaimed. "Here's more water. Drink it, okay?"

She fed the bear the fish and while he ate slowly, he seemed to relish every morsel. Baldie then set his head down beside the bowl, exhausted. If he kept improving Jane would undo the rope in the morning to set the bear free. He was eating, had water to drink, and she could leave extra food.

And once the bear realized he was free, he'd go down to the river to drink.

The next morning she returned with more fish and water, letting the bear have his fill. Once the fish had disappeared opened a couple cans of Spam, placing it on the ground away from him. She wanted to force him to get up. She went to his back leg and removed the rope, but once she did the bear got up and hobbled painfully to the trees, ignoring the canned meat. Nerves on full alert, Jane untied the rope from the tree and calmly backed out of the clearing. Calling Sam in a quiet voice, she steeled herself to not to take off running. Baldie stopped long enough to watch her until she was out of sight in the trees leading down the hill to the river. Her heart ached for the bear that had once been her friend. She hoped he'd recover.

It wasn't until she was at camp that she realized how fast her heart was beating. She broke camp and started packing up. The horses seemed more than anxious to leave this mysterious place. Charlie had to act like a knot head as usual, giving a few bucks as she settled into the saddle, but this time Jane was ready. He soon settled down and threw himself into the work, taking up the trial once again and leading Misty. Sam ran alongside, barking crazily, just happy to be on their way.

It had taken Jane 10 days to get to the Cadott and she had stayed two days helping the bear. They were a bit behind schedule but she could make up the time spent with the bear. The trail wasn't too bad as long as she stayed on it but she knew that to wander off a bit meant risking a tumble down a 100-foot sheer cliff into the river. In some places the canyons were steep and rather dangerous, but the trip was exhilarating. Jane sometimes wondered why people travelled to other places for vacations when they had all the beauty in the world right there in their own backyard.

But as she made her way in the coming days, Jane couldn't quite shake the eerie sensation she was being followed. She didn't like the feeling, and she liked it even less when Sam made it clear by his steady low growl, and his frequent looking back, that he too sensed something was amiss.

"Bet it's a bear or wolf stalking us," she said to Sam. She knew this in itself was a serious enough matter because bears and wolves usually did their best to avoid people. They didn't like confrontations with humans. Only a very hungry bear or wolf would throw caution to the wind to stalk a human. Pulling her rifle from its scabbard she decided to ride the rest of the way with it across her lap.

Finally, she came emerged from the bush. In front of her lay the flats, acres of neat farmland stretching miles in front of her and surrounded by the river. She knew this area well. Not too far ahead was an old trapper's cabin where she could stay the night. She was relieved to finally reach her destination, unable to shake the uneasiness that had followed her all afternoon. The horses seemed to share her contentment as Jane watered them before tethering them and allowing them to graze away the rest of the day. She made her way down to the river to fetch water for the cabin, pausing along the way to admire the beauty of the river, the cliffs, and the hills. She spotted some boats on the river but the foliage of the trees was too thick for them to be able to see her. As she worked her way down to the river, she saw a cow moose come out of the shore bushes with her spring calf. They walked boldly into the river, where they had a drink and a swim to cool off from the heat of the day.

Jane rubbed the back of her neck uneasily. She couldn't shake the feeling that she was being watched. "I hate this!" she said out loud. "I hate being afraid of something I can't see." Filling the billy tin, she called Sam and headed uphill, knowing she would be safe for the night in the cabin. She left Sam outside to guard the horses. "If you hear anything," she told her faithful friend, "you just bark your fool old head off and I'll be right out! Okay?" The dog licked her hand and reluctantly settled down for the night.

The next morning they rose early and got off to a good start. Jane figured another two or three days and they would be at the White Mud. The day was gloomy with low clouds. "Going to rain again," thought Jane, "and that wind has a chill to it. Come on you guys. Get the lead out. Time to get moving."

Around noon Jane found a creek that ran into the Peace where she stopped to do some fishing. She and Sam would have fish for supper. It was a nice quiet spot, so Jane decided to camp for the night. Unpacking Misty, she tethered the horses so they could graze. Then she cleaned and cooked the fish and she and Sam ate their fill.

Jane heard thunder in the distance, and looking at the sky saw black clouds closing in. "Well Sam, looks like we're in for a mean thunderstorm. Too bad we aren't back at the cabin."

She quickly set up her little tent and shoved the rifle and bedroll inside. She gathered dry wood for the fire and placed it in a corner of the tent. "If this keeps up, Sam, we'll need a bigger tent." She brought in the saddle to serve as a pillow; everything else could survive a soaking. Lightning raced across the black sky in the distance as the rumbling thunder closed in. It wasn't long before the storm was on top of them and jagged lightning striking from sky to earth. Soon the rain came in such thick sheets it was impossible to see across the clearing.

It was cosy in the tent with Sam cuddled close to her. He hated thunder and was happy to hide behind his mistress on the bedroll. As the storm blew itself out, Jane fell asleep, only to be violently awakened by screams from the horses and Sam trying to get out of the tent. She unzipped the flaps and Sam scrambled out, running at breakneck speed toward the horses. Jane grabbed the rifle and followed. She almost choked on the lump of fear that jumped into her throat, seeing that a bear was attacking her helpless horses.

Misty's tether stake came out of the ground and she took off, running as though all the demons of hell were behind her. Jane aimed her rifle and fired. The grizzly let louse a scream of pain. Charlie slipped and fallen on the wet grass trying to escape the bear. But he regained his footing in a flash, gave his tether stake another powerful pull, and jerked it free. Jane was shocked to see the horse turn on the bear with bared teeth and flailing hooves rather than trying to make his escape. Charlie and Sam had the grizzly going in circles, making another shot impossible. Jane would have to wait until Charlie moved away. But before she could fire off a shot, the grizzly screamed out again as a hoof thudded into its head. The grizzly spun like a dancer and took off into the bush with the dog and horse in close pursuit. Whistling as hard as she could and calling to Sam, Jane hurried to follow them into the trees. She couldn't see a thing but she could hear Sam howling in the deep brush as he searched for the bear. After calling for a few more minutes, Jane started back to the tent, but froze when she heard a deep-throated growl behind her. The grizzly had circled back and was just a few yards away.

Stepping back in surprise, Jane tripped and landed on her back, the rifle flying out of her hands. The bear rose on its back legs, roaring and staring her down angrily. Jerking to her knees, Jane grabbed the rifle, aimed and fired in one fluid motion. She quickly cocked the gun again and fired as the bear kept coming at her. Scrambling desperately to get to her feet, she stumbled and ran towards the tent having emptied the last round. Fortunately, she knew exactly where the box of shells was and she grabbed a handful out of the tent in record time. Gluing her eyes to the slowly approaching bear—now in full stalking mode—she shoved the shells into the clip as fast as she could, her hands trembling so violently she could barely hold the rifle. The first three bullets had slowed him but he was still advancing, albeit somewhat unsteadily.

Jane fired. Shaking his big head, the grizzly staggered. Cocking and firing again Jane held her ground and the big bear went down on his front knees. But still he advanced. Aiming once again with her last shot Jane exclaimed, "God, please help me!" and fired again. The bear fell at her feet, shuddering in an attempt to get up once again. Stepping back, Jane pulled the remaining bullets from her pocket and, hands trembling, jammed them into the clip and fired three more bullets into the brute's head.

She couldn't believe how lucky she'd been after stupidly chasing a grizzly into brush without a single spare shell. But she couldn't help but wonder where the bear had come from. This wasn't grizzly country. She'd seen plenty of bears in the area, but never a grizzly. Jane buried her head in her hands. She could just hear her father's voice calling out her stupidity, "Janie, how many times did I tell you? Always keep extra bullets in your pocket. Weren't you listening Janie?" This fiasco would not have impressed him.

But now she knew what had been stalking them for the last few days. She wondered how many times the bear had come close to mauling them. Shuddering, she remembered Sam's frequent growling.

"Yeah, yeah, Sam...I should've listened to you when you ran off barking. Okay, Sam, now where the hell are you? Do I have to go and find you in the bush? Hope that bear didn't rip you apart."

Some guard dog! He's running around in the bush after nothing now. She walked over to the edge of the forest and heard the faint sound of Sam yipping and barking.

"Squirrels!" She laughed until her sides hurt and she couldn't breathe, the relief that the danger had passed sweeping over her. "Oh my, that was just too close for comfort," she sighed, wiping tears from her face.

But as quickly as the sense of relief had hit her, it was gone. Jane knew she had a problem, a big one. She was at least three or four days away from the White Mud and without a horse. If she could just reach the White Mud there would be people there to help her. So Jane went back to her tent, sorting out what she could take with her on foot. Two or three days on horseback meant at least five or six days on foot. She had to pack light and make sure she took only what was most important: the small axe, the side cutters, and the bedroll. Not including the rifle, she would have close to 40 pounds on her back. Her saddle and everything else she left behind she'd put in the tent and come back for once she had a horse. She took a bridle just in case she ran into one of them.

She was almost done organizing everything when Sam finally returned. Spotting the grizzly on the ground, he went ballistic until he finally realized it was no longer a threat. Jane rolled her eyes, "Oh the great and mighty protector returneth! What were you chasing out there? Squirrels and shadows? How did you get so confused? He was behind you!" Taking a can of stew and some crackers, she ate before hitting the road, Sam's eyes watching her every bite.

Back in town, the RCMP was going in circles trying to track the fugitives. Having presumed the criminals were headed north to High Level, they had alerted the High Level Police Detachment to watch for anyone unusual. They had the licence number and description of the stolen vehicle but the North being such a vast area the men could easily disappear anywhere. Their biggest concern was the safety of the little boy, Devon. They alerted Peace and North Country officials to be on the lookout for an abandoned child or for two men with a little boy.

Constable Mark Snyder had only been with the police force for two years and this case bothered him terribly. He had a four-year-old son of his own, Adam, at home and every time he thought about Devon, he couldn't help but think of his own boy.

Did the criminals stay on the main highways or had they disappeared into the bush? If they were hiding in the bush somewhere, God help that little boy. Mark was sure they had only taken the boy as a possible hostage if needed, so he knew that once the men felt they were free and clear that time would run out for the little fellow.

That night, as Mark lay listening to his wife's soft breathing, he challenged himself, to get into the mind of someone who was on the run. *Would he head to Edmonton or Calgary?* NO, there would be check stops everywhere for weeks, they had to know that. *How about north to High Level and the Northwest Territories?* No, still too risky for them.

Just as Mark rolled over and wrapped his arms around his wife, he had a brainwave. *I wouldn't go south and I wouldn't go north! I'd find a place smack-dab in the middle of nowhere and get lost for a while. When the heat's off, then I'd make my move for freedom.* Trying to stay ahead of the oncoming waves of sleep, he wondered, *Where would I go to get lost?*

"Toward a river," a tiny voice seemed to say as his eyes closed in sleep.

Mark woke up early the next morning for his shift. As he headed for the shower, he could hear his wife fixing coffee. He looked in on their sleeping child. Tousled brown hair framed the flushed face of the sleeping boy. Leaning down, he kissed the little guy's cheek and the child stirred and opened his eyes.

"Hi Daddy," he said as he reached up to touch his father's face.

Mark kissed him again, "Love ya, buddy."

"Me love you too, Daddy," the little boy said as he closed his eyes and went back to sleep.

Adam was a livewire and kept his mother on the run. Mark smiled to himself to think of some of the stories his wife had told him about his antics. Working the shifts he did, there wasn't a lot of time to spend with Adam, but thinking about another little boy just like him, at the mercy of those men tugged at his heartstrings. *Dear God, I hope you're keeping Devon alive. Please help me find him. I need all the help I can get.*

As he sat down with his wife he shared his thoughts on the case with Andrea, "You know, Andi, I was thinking about those two despicable guys and that little boy last night. Just couldn't get to sleep. I just can't figure out where they went."

"Mark," Andrea said, "you know they could be close by here. There are lots of cabins all along the Peace. Talk about perfect hideouts! And not many people out there with all this rain. Those guys could hide in a cabin with no problem. Now finish your toast and coffee, Mr. Sleuth, and get looking!"

She kissed him goodbye with a twinkle in her eye and after she heard the slam of car door she did something she couldn't remember doing before: she locked the front door.

Cam was at his Ottawa desk when fellow homicide detective Mitch Gates stopped by with some papers. "Cam, these papers just came through from Alberta. Might interest you."

"Yeah?" said Cam. "What's up?"

"Remember the other day, you were working on that Simon Drosset homicide and you found it wasn't Drosset?"

"Yeah, yeah. Still working on that one. Finally figured out who the dead guy was."

"Okay, how'd you do that?" Mitch asked.

"We got a report from an auxiliary hospital staffer who was looking for the son of a Mrs. Iona Ladour. This woman took a turn for the worse in her nursing home and they were trying to locate her son. When she died her whole estate was frozen until they could find him, so they filed a missing persons report."

"When I went to the hospital, they gave me a picture of the son. And you wouldn't believe it, Mitch, he's a dead ringer for Simon Drosset, and of course the birthmark was a match. So I closed that part of my case but I followed the money withdrawals from Ladour's bank account and wouldn't you know, there was one in Alberta. Of course, once the bank account got frozen, no one came forward to complain. But I'm pretty sure that we're looking for Simon Drosset posing as Guy Ladour."

"Well then, you're gonna love this," Mitch said. "You're on the right track. A little town in Alberta called Peace River, way up north, had a prison break where two security guards were killed. Two guys escaped to a little town about 60 miles further north and almost killed a young couple and kidnapped their kid."

"So...what's the connection?" asked Guy.

"The clincher is," said Mitch, "that a 'Guy Ladour' with a solid resume was hired at the prison there, where he worked for a couple of months. It just so happened there was a prisoner there named Kip Drosset and they're sure this Kip escaped with inside help. Whoever helped him had to know the layout of the prison, schedules, everything."

"Bingo!" Cam said. "Simon Drosset is alive and well. Thanks, Mitch, I'll talk to the sergeant and see about heading out to Alberta. Drosset's a far more dangerous man than they can imagine and I'm afraid before this is over there'll be more bodies in his wake."

Cam practically sprinted over to the sergeant's office and knocked on the door. He motioned him in. "Hey, Cam, come in. What've you got for me?"

Cam explained everything he knew about the Guy Ladour homicide, the Kip Drosset prison break, and how he knew that Simon Drosset was posing as Guy Ladour.

Sergeant Matta listened with interest, "So you plan to head to Alberta, I take it?"

"Yeah," said Cam. "What do you think?"

"I think it's a go," he said as he picked up the phone. "I'll make some travel arrangements and you get on the horn to let Peace River know you're coming. I'm sure they'd be happy for the extra help, with everything that's happening up there."

Before he knew it Cam was en route for Peace River country with a complete dossier on the Drosset brothers. He was met by Corporal Lane Malone at the Peace River Airport, Corporal and after introductions and a quick bite they set upon the work at hand. The two pored over every shred of evidence on the crimes.

"Lane, what do you think? Did these guys go up north?" Cam asked.

"No," the Corporal said, "I don't think they got by us. My take is that they are either in the community or not far away."

As he talked, Cam watched the corporal's broad shoulders slump, "I just hope to hell that little boy is still alive. I love my job but when kids are involved, I hate every minute of it."

Cam agreed with the gentle-hearted cop. It was a part of his job he hated as well, but as long as no body turned up there was still hope.

Cam headed to Manning in the morning, only to find the detachment in an uproar. One of the town's three officers, Constable Mark Snyder, had disappeared the night before and had not been heard from since.

After introductions, Cam inquired, "Have you talked to Snyder's wife?"

Corporal Brian Stevens nodded and said she had phoned into the office the evening before, wondering if he was working overtime. They had scoured the community, checked his paperwork and schedule, and come up empty.

"Mind if we drive over and talk with his wife?" Cam asked. "Maybe he said something to her that she it didn't occur to her to mention to you."

Corporal Stevens agreed and set his remaining constable, Ray Merriam, to the task of escorting Cam to the Snyder residence.

It was 10 in the morning when they arrived at the Snyders'. Cam stood a moment, looking over the well-kept yard with a swing set creaking in the wind. There was a sandbox to the side with a little dump truck and tractors. As they approached the front door it opened before they even had a chance to knock.

"Ray! Did you find him?"

Cam figured the petite blonde hadn't slept all night. Anxiety showed all over her delicate features.

"No, Andi. I'm sorry. Nothing. Haven't heard a thing," Ray said apologetically. "This is Detective Cam Jansen from Ottawa. He's helping us with the case. He wants to ask you some questions."

"Why...why of course. Come in. Please come in." Andi motioned them in. "Coffee? And pardon the way I look, I just can't get myself going today."

A little boy appeared behind her and Ray greeted him, "Morning, Adam. How're you doing today?"

"My daddy didn't come home and my mommy's crying. Can you find him and tell him to come home?"

"Sure can, Adam," Ray said as he swept the little boy up into his arms. "The minute I see him I'll tell him to come home right away and give you a big hug just like this."

Looking at Cam he said, "You talk to Andi and I'll take Adam out in the yard."

Cam nodded and followed Andrea to the kitchen as Ray headed outside with the child. As she poured coffee Cam began his inquiry, "Did Mark mention what was on his mind or where he thought he'd be going yesterday?"

Andrea nodded, "We were talking about the rental cabins that line rivers and that maybe it would be a good place for those fugitives to hide. He didn't think they had left the area, he figured they might be hiding around here. But I don't know what river or what cabin he was going to investigate. We have the Notikewin River close to town, and to the north there's the Second and Third Battle Rivers. And east of the town there's the Peace River, but it extends for miles and miles. There are cabins along the banks of all these rivers, so I have no idea where he might have been headed."

Cam nodded. It wasn't much, but it was enough to start with. He thanked Andrea for the coffee, and took his leave. As he looked back at the doorway it broke his heart to see the forlorn young mother standing in the doorway with the little boy in her arms.

"Ray...we've just got to find him," Cam said as they left.

"Yeah, I know," grunted Ray.

Back at the detachment, Cam informed the men of his findings and they set out on a search of all the cabins in the areas surrounding the rivers. They started out to check the Battle Rivers area and sent out a warning on the radio to cabin inhabitants in the region to be on their guard.

Jane knew her enjoyment of the walk along the bottom of the hills by the river would be short-lived. Soon she would be climbing hills that might as well have been cliffs. She started the long climb and grabbed her dog's collar to help get him moving, "Come on, Sam. We can do it." They rested briefly as they neared the summit, "Hot isn't it, Sam? I figure we're about five miles from the White Mud. We can rest there, hit the highway, and catch a ride back to Manning."

She knew that if the horses came showed up without her, and could be identified, then in all likelihood a search party would be mounted. She shook her head, half in disgust, half in frustration, knowing that the police had enough to do without chasing after idiots like her who'd lost their horses. "Come on, pup. Best get going. Sitting here won't get the job done."

The route continued its up-and-down convolutions, but abruptly the sharp hills transformed into rolling knolls. She was happy to follow a faint game trail that brought them closer to the White Mud and its cabins. As she pushed through the dense bush, Sam, who had run ahead, stopped suddenly and growled. He looked back at her as if waiting for instructions before turning back towards a pile of brush. Her rifle at the ready, Jane carefully and quietly inched closer, not knowing if the dog had found a fawn, another bear, or something dead. By now, Sam's head had burrowed into the branches and his low growls had changed into eager whines and frantic tail-wagging. Thoroughly confused, Jane used the rifle barrel to move a leafy branch aside. Her heart stopped. Lying on the ground, clutching a tattered blanket, was a sleeping boy with bloodied feet. Tears had streaked his dirty face and with every other breath he drew a ragged sigh. He awoke with a jerk and emitted a squeak of alarm.

"Don't worry little guy. I won't hurt you."

A wild look of fear flared in his eyes, but was quickly replaced by tears as Jane offered her hand to help him out of the bush. She embraced him and picked him up. "I want my mommy, where's my mommy?"

Tears flooded Jane's eyes as she comforted him, "I'll take you to your mommy, don't worry. We'll find her."

Holding the child like a china doll, Jane walked to the river where she soaked his feet and washed his face.

Looking up at her, he whispered, "I'm really hungry."

"I have some nice stew in my pack, we'll go get it." She picked him up and carried him over to her pack. It was a long shot, but she asked anyway, "Is your name Devon?"

He nodded, "I seen you in town. The horse lady."

"Yes," Jane said, "that's me. How did you get way up here?"

"The bad mans took me and I runned away. I've been here a long long time, a hundred days. I was scared of the dark but the mans kept yelling at me. And they hurt me."

The little boy flinched as Jane set him down.

"Where do you hurt, honey?"

"The bad mans hurt my arm."

Moving his pyjama top, Jane winced as she saw black and blue finger marks embedded in the child's arm. She was

BEVERLY LEIN

pretty sure his collarbone was broken by the way he held his arm against his side. "Okay, honey. You just take it easy and I'll get you something to eat." As she fumbled through her pack, she raged under her breath, "The dirty sons of bitches, I'll …"

The child's whimpering shifted her attention back to his injuries. She removed her kerchief and used it to secure his arm to his body. "There you go, Devon. That should help. Maybe it won't hurt so much." Not wanting to bother with a fire, she fed Devon the stew straight out of the can. He gobbled it down without so much as a word.

Jane said, "Devon, where are the bad men now?"

"Don't know. Over there. I walked long way from the mans."

"Let's be real quiet just in case they hear us," whispered Jane. "We don't want them to find us, do we?" She stretched out her bedroll and when Devon had finished eating, he cuddled into her arms, holding onto her tightly as though he was afraid she would disappear if he didn't hold on to her with all his might. As he fell asleep and she tucked him into the bedroll. Jane ordered Sam to stay with the sleeping child and started toward the cabins, gun at the ready, slipping silently through the trees.

She hadn't gone far when she spotted the string of cabins with nestled almost invisibly back behind the trees. As she closed in she noticed a police car parked in front. Heaving a sigh of relief she abandoned her crouch and started to walk boldly from out of the trees. Then she heard yelling. An officer had his gun pointed at someone in front of the car, telling him man to lie down. Jane quickly stepped back into the trees and watched in horror as another man snuck up from behind and hit the officer on the head. Jane's eyes widened

43

and her sharp intake of breath was so loud she feared the men would hear. But they were focused on their prey and Jane watched helplessly as they pitched the unconscious policeman into the cruiser. Jumping into the driver's seat, one of the men began driving towards her, heading for the riverbank. Scampering further into the trees, Jane watched the man jump out just in time to avoid accompanying the car into the river.

He's going to drown! Jane saw the men watch the vehicle disappear into the water and then gleefully head back to the cabin. Jane ran to the edge of the bank, being sure to stay hidden in the trees. She could barely see the last of the police car disappearing into the water. She ran down the steep riverbank and quickly dove in knowing there was no time to waste; the car was going down so fast and she was losing sight of it. By the time she reached it, water had already filled the interior of the cruiser. Reaching through the open window, she got a grip of the man's arm. Her breath running low, she pulled him closer to the window, reached around until she found the back of his shirt, and pulling with all her might, got him halfway through the window. But something was holding him back. Out of air, she shot to the surface, gasped twice, and plunged under again. Grabbing the officer's trunk with all the strength she had, she pulled at him but he stayed stuck and Jane had to go up for air again. She gulped and then quickly submerged to continue her struggle. Reaching beyond his knees into the car she found his foot was stuck in the steering wheel. Tugging hard she finally managed to wrench it free, grabbed him by the collar, and pulled him toward the surface, her lungs screaming for air.

I'm not going to make it. She was forced to let go of the man and claw her way back to the surface. With one last desperate gasp of air she dove back down one more time. The current was strong and he had drifted into the murky water. More by touch than by sight, she found him. With all that was left of her strength, she hauled him to the surface. After manoeuvring the big man to the shore, she pinned her body against his and tried to breathe into his mouth. After a few moments of what seemed like eternity, she pulled herself from the water, dragged him up on the bank beside her, and tried to push him onto his side to expel the water in his lungs. She was badly winded after nearly losing him to the current and she struggled roll him over. She breathed into his mouth she tried once more to breathe into his mouth.

"Come on, come on! Breathe, damn it! Don't die on me!"

Just as she was ready to give up, he coughed heavily and vomited a significant amount of water. Jane finally found the strength to turn him onto his side, and then onto his stomach. She pumped on his back until he stopped coughing water. Retching and gagging, he fought to draw air into his tortured lungs.

"Oh God, Oh God, please help him breathe!" Jane cried. "Come on, man, you're going to make it." Groaning with exertion, she rolled him onto his side again and helped him sit up.

"What happened?" he croaked, looking at Jane. "Who are you?"

"Jane," she said. "You got nailed on the head and they dumped you in the river. I only just managed to pull you out."

"Well, thanks..."

"Don't talk now. Save your strength and let's get you up. We've got to hide. They might come back."

Slipping in the mud and working with what was left of her strength, Jane helped the officer to his feet. They staggered ahead ever so slowly, barely making it up the steep riverbank. As they neared to the top Jane paused, "Wait here. I'll get my rifle."

"Yeah, sure," mumbled the exhausted officer. "How do I..." but she wasn't listening. He dropped his hand to his holster. "Be careful," he croaked, "they got my gun."

"Probably did," Jane said as she left. "Stay low and I'll be right back."

She found her rifle and spotted the two men standing outside the cabin, drinking from a liquor bottle. Their rough laughter floated across the open area, loud enough to cause her to immediately flatten herself into the long grass. She wriggled slowly out of their line of sight and backed into the trees as the men turned back towards the riverbank. Holding the rifle tightly, she was glad she had moved the policeman back from the bank and into the bush. Cautiously edging back to where she'd left him, she found him in a semi-conscious state.

"Come on, man. Get up. We've got to get out of here." After a moments she was able to rouse him into a half-sitting position and slowly she half-dragged, half-carried him deeper into the bush.

"W-w-where are we going?" the officer mumbled, collapsing over.

"There's a place up ahead," she said. "It's safe."

Setting down the rifle, she gently pushed the man to safety underneath the covering branches the bushes with Devon.

Now I'm really up the creek, she thought, *two helpless people on my hands.*

There had to be a way for her to alert the authorities to what was going on out here. She grabbed the old stew can, cleaned it out, and quickly drafted a note detailing their location and the situation. She signed and dated it, wedged it carefully into the tin, and carefully strapped it on to Sam's heavy leather collar.

She hugged the dog closely whispering into his ear, "Go Sam. Go back home!" The devoted collie began to whine. "Go! Go back home, Sam!" Find Marcy. Get help, Sam!"

Sam cocked his head in recognition and started to leave, stopped. He stopped briefly, looking back at his mistress, but the tone in Jane's voice was unmistakable—it was urgent and it was serious.

Cam and the other officers searched cabins along the Notikewin and Battle Rivers over for four days. They checked Weasel's Park and Sunny Valley. Nothing. On the fifth day, Cam announced, "I'm going to Peace River and see what the boys have turned up there. Maybe they got something or have come up with some different ideas."

"Yeah, whatever," Ray said, almost too tired to care. "You do that. See you in a couple days, okay? And don't go home without calling us."

"Don't worry," said Cam, "I'll keep in touch."

As he drove out of the town, he couldn't help but admire the beautiful countryside. Even with the cloudy sky touching the green of the trees, it was spectacular. When the sun broke through the clouds, the blue sky almost sparkled in the distance. He was so admiring the landscape that he nearly missed the sign for White Mud. He spotted it out of the corner of his eye, slammed on the brakes and backed up.

Hadn't someone at the office mentioned the White Mud and cabins? In no hurry to get to Peace River, Cam turned down the well-graded road. As he headed down the road he knew in his gut that Mark had found the killers—what he didn't know was if he'd survived the encounter. He couldn't bring himself to think about what had happened to the little boy.

As he drove up to a set of cabins he saw a man walking toward him. The sun in his face, he rolled down the window, "Howdy, neighbour. You own one of the cabins around here?"

"Sure do fella," the man replied. "Who wants to know?"

"I'm just passing through," Cam said, "I heard what a nice place the White Mud is and thought I'd take a look."

As the man neared Cam was hit by a moment of recognition: without a doubt he was looking at Simon Drosset.

Shielding his emotions, he engaged the man further, "Sure could use a cup of coffee if you got one handy. Maybe you got something I could rent."

"Got nothin' to rent, but the coffee's on. Follow me," he responded and led Cam toward a cabin nestled back in the trees. Looking around, Cam didn't see a police car but knew they could easily have hidden it. As they entered the cabin, a younger man jumped off a bunk, exclaiming, "What the hell?"

"Relax, we got company is all. Buddy here is looking for a cup of coffee. So what's your name, stranger?"

"Cam Jensen, all the way from Ontario. Just taking a little holiday. What about you guys? You from around here?"

"No, no. We're not from around here. We're from Ontario too. We're the Ladour brothers, Simon and Kip, and we're just passing through, just like you."

"Glad to make your acquaintance," Cam said without blinking an eye. "You guys come here every year for holidays?"

Simon's eyes narrowed as he looked at Cam and said, "You sure ask a lot of questions for a stranger."

"Hey, sorry, sorry!" said Cam. "Sorry for sounding so nosy. Didn't mean to offend."

As he scanned the cabin, Cam tried to hide his anger when couldn't see any trace of Devon. *The bastards have killed him or abandoned him in the bush.* And if Mark had ever been here, there was no sign of him now.

Finishing his coffee Cam said, "Well, I'll be getting on. Thanks for the coffee, but I'd better be making a mile. Glad to meet you guys. Maybe I'll find a place to rent up the road." As he stood up to leave, Simon said, "I don't think you'll be going anywhere 'cause we need your car."

Cam turned slowly to face the man behind him. Still playing dumb, he said, "You need to borrow my car?"

"No, dummy," Simon said, "...not borrow. We're taking it like."

Eyes narrowed, Simon backhanded Cam across the face. "I hate people who are hard of hearing," he said as Cam staggered backwards, falling against the table.

Kip grabbed Cam's arms from behind as Simon searched his pockets, pulling out his wallet. Yanking the coat open he said, "Well, lookie, lookie. Ain't this somethin'?"

He pulled Cam's gun from its shoulder holster. "Nice touch buddy-boy. We'll just have to make it look like you shot yourself before we leave." Reaching into another pocket, he pulled out Cam's police department badge.

"Well, well, what have we got here. We got us a homicide detective guy. And just who would you be looking for mister homicide officer boy?"

The two men threw their heads back laughing at their own wit before Simon continued, "I guess you're looking for us, the famous Drosset brothers, eh? You guys finally figured out who I was, didn't you? But you're too damn smart for your own good."

Cam was done playing dumb, "I made you the second I saw you. Your resemblance to Guy Ladour really is remarkable, isn't it? You killed the poor bastard, didn't you?"

Simon chuckled, "And how long did it take you numbskulls to figure that out?"

"We were stuck for nearly three months, until your cousin's wife set us straight."

"That little bitch has caused me tons of trouble over the years. One of these days I'm gonna pay her a cousinly visit."

A chill ran down Cam's back hearing the venom in the man's voice. Pushing Cam roughly to the floor, Simon used Cam's own handcuffs to secure him to the bedrail.

Kip pulled the handcuff keys out of Cam's pocket,, "Hey Simon, we can't forget the cuff keys. Can't leave 'em here with Officer Wise Guy can we?"

And with that Cam breathed a small sigh of relief; the brothers had neglected to search him carefully. If they had looked closer, they would have found a spare handcuff key taped under one of his socks and a derringer sitting in an ankle holster. He realized that with both hands cuffed to the bed, he had a real problem, but...

The evening was cold and rain began falling around eight o'clock. Mark needed help desperately blood oozed from his head where he had been so savagely hit. He was cold beneath the sleeping bag and the shirt that Jane had taken off him would not dry without a fire.

Devon snuggled closer to Jane for warmth. The bedroll, which she had tried tucking around all three of them, just wasn't enough. She knew it was safer to wait until dark before raiding a cabin for blankets, first aid, and food. She was terrified that if the killers caught her, the boy and the man would die.

As the rain turned into a downpour, the branches protected them less and less. Pushing Devon gently away from her, she told him, "You stay here by the policeman. I'm going to cover the top of the pile with more branches."

Jane stepped into the rain with her hatchet, thankful for her slicker. After chopping off some spruce branches, she piled them in a crisscross pattern over top of their makeshift hideaway. By time she crawled back in, she was thoroughly chilled but the branches did seem to be halting some of the rain. She knew their shelter would do little to protect the officer—they were in desperate need of blankets. The officer was trembling uncontrollably but Jane decided to wait until Devon fell asleep before foraging for supplies.

Once the boy was slumbering she gently shook the young police officer, "Hey, wake up." Mark shook himself out of his stupor when he heard her calling. She said, "Tell me your name!"

Trying to get his swollen tongue around his words, he mumbled, "Mark. Can you call the detach..."His words faded into a jumble. "Water. Can I have some water? I'm so thirsty."

Jane gave him a small swallow. "My head is killing me ... oh, it hurts ... it hurts real bad."

"Hey. Listen up, Mark. Mark! Pay attention!" Jane had to grab his face and firmly turn him towards to focus. "I'm going for more blankets and food but I have to leave you with the boy. You watch Devon and if he wakes up, don't let him leave or make any noise, okay?"

"Yeah, well, yeah. Okay," Mark mumbled. "Yeah. Blankets, okay. Where's that dog? Is he yours or theirs?"

"He's mine," said Jane, "and I sent him home. It's a long shot, but maybe he'll find someone to bring back help. Mark ... I know you're hurt real bad, but you have to fight. I'll try to find some first aid stuff. But if I get caught, you're on your own with Devon. I think you're a bit stronger now, and if you have to leave here, you need to go to your left. You've got about 10 miles until you'll hit a road where there a houses. If something happens to me, you're Devon's only hope."

Mark nodded and groaned, "I'll do my best."

As she crept out of their shelter and into the rain, Jane shivered. *Maybe I should just walk the 10 miles to the road and leave them. No, that's dumb. I've got to get blankets or they're going to die.* She carefully pushed through the bush, keeping well away from the cabin. She wished she had brought her rifle with her but she'd had no choice—Mark needed it more than she did. Besides, she needed her hands free to carry whatever she could find. Creeping through the trees, she circled even further away from the commandeered cabin and headed for the group of cabins closer to the riverbank. The darkness made it difficult to see but stumbling along steadily, she reached the first cabin in less than half-an-hour. As luck would have it, it was cabin that belonged to friends of hers and she knew where they'd hidden the extra key.

She quickly let herself in, struck a match, and began rummaging through the cupboards for canned food. From the propane fridge she found some wieners and buns, using a heavy quilt from the bed as a carry bag. She moved her search on and located a first aid kit, placing it with into the middle of the quilt with the other treasures. She twisted the corners of the quilt and hoisted it to her shoulder.

Jane slipped back into the rainy night and reached the brush pile without mishap. She cleaned Mark's wound before soaking it with iodine. "Here, Mark," she said. "I found some Aspirin. Take two. Here's some water."

Cutting one of the pills in half, she gave one to Devon in the hopes of easing his runny nose and cough. Then, opening a can of beans, she spoon-fed Mark, breaking off little pieces of wiener for him. He kept them down for only 15 minutes, his worsening condition increasing her worry. After giving Devon some cold soup she tucked the big quilt around the three of them and waited for morning.

When Jane woke she told Mark she was going to check if the men had left. She was hoping against hope that they had, so at least Mark and Devon could be moved to the safety and warmth of the cabin—if the rain kept falling it was unlikely that anyone else would come up to the cabins for several days.

Leaving the gun with Mark, she crept toward the cabin. Through the drizzle she saw smoke from the chimney. "The bastards are still here," she cursed. But now there was a maroon car in the driveway. Jane wondered if they had another accomplice or if another unsuspecting victim had come across their path. Sneaking up behind the cabin, Jane crept below a window. It was open just a crack, but inside she could hear men talking.

"After two weeks the cops will still be watching for that blue van."

"Ya got that right. But they wouldn't be lookin' for no fancy rental car."

Lifting her head, Jane peeked into the cabin and saw the men with their backs to her, drinking coffee. A short distance from them she saw a man on the floor with his hands shackled to a bed. Her heart pounded as she heard them address the man on the floor.

"Well, copper, not exactly your all-round smartest day, was it? You just walked into our arms so smooth and easy-like. Yessir, it was right sweet and purdy. Now that you are in the lion's den, what you gonna do?"

Jane seethed. What the hell was with these cops sending one lone cop at a time down here? And who was this guy anyway? *They should have sent a whole army of cops*, she raged to herself. Her heart fell as reality hit her: if these cops had come out here on their own then it was likely nobody knew they were out here at all.

It was late afternoon when Jake Willans, the farmer that rented Jane's land, spotted two horses wandered the fields around the property.

"What's with them horses?" his wife, Flo, asked. "Aren't they Jane's?"

Jake saw the forlorn-looking animals, mud splattered and looking beat-up. "That's kind of screwy," he said. "Just a minute, we better check this." He pulled the truck around towards the yard and hopped out, walking closer to the horses.

"Honey, you get the corral opened," Jake yelled back, "and I'll go check the house. Hurry!"

He ran to the house and banged on the door, but it was locked: something had happened to Jane. Running back to the horses, he chased them into the corral. They quickly gave them some oats and water, secured them in their stalls, and then raced towards town.

The rain was pouring down as Marcy, stood on her farmhouse veranda wondering how Jane was making out. She couldn't do much outside when it rained like this, so she decided it would be a good time to visit her mother. Just as she was about to head back in spotted what looked like a wolf in distance heading down her driveway. As it came closer she realized it was a dog. Once it had reached the top of the driveway Marcy realized that the drenched animal was Jane's collie, Sam. Jumping off the steps, she ran through the rain toward the dog. "Sam! What are you doing here?"

The dishevelled dog barked a weak greeting, rubbing his wet body against her bare legs. "Okay, okay Sam. And where are Jane and the horses?" She looked through the driving rain and saw nothing but an empty road. "Where's Jane, Sam?"

The dog barked sharply at the sound of his mistress' name and that's when Marcy saw the tin can slung under his neck. Worry hit her like a heavy weight as she grabbed Sam's collar and pulled him up onto the veranda. With fumbling hands she removed the collar and dug into the can. Jane's note, although thoroughly soaked, was still inside and still legible.

Marcy raced for the car with the dog on her heels. The gravel flew out from under her tires as Marcy spun out of the yard.

Corporal Brian Stevens watched the rain pound down over Manning. Rubbing his forehead, he wondered aloud, "Funny that Lane hasn't phoned down from Peace River with anything."

"Yeah, I was wondering about that too," said Ray from across the office. "And what about that Cam? He was supposed to keep in contact with us!"

Brian nodded. "Maybe something came up and he got busy with a lead."

"Yeah, probably," said Ray, "but we're going to need more help around here, Corporal. Without Mark there just aren't enough of us to tackle this job."

Brian sighed and wiped his tired eyes with his hands. "Right again, Ray. I called HQ for more hands, but it's taking longer than they expected to get bodies together and out to us."

Picking up the phone, he dialled up Corporal Lane Malone: "So how's Detective Jensen making out with you guys?"

There was dead silence on the phone for a moment before Lane responded, "Cam Jensen? The guy from Ottawa? He went to see you guys. Didn't he get there?"

"Yeah, he was here," said Brian, "but he left to go back to Peace River to see you guys. Been gone a couple of days now."

"Well, he never showed up here!" Lane exclaimed.

"What? No…Really? We haven't seen or heard from him since he left Manning. Didn't he call you guys or anything?"

"He's not here and we haven't heard a thing from him," Lane repeated, almost automatically. "Don't tell me we got another man missing?"

Before the news of Cam's disappearance could sink in, the Manning detachment door flew open and Jake practically fell through the door in his excitement.

"Hey, Brian! We've got us a problem!" he cried as he approached the counter with Flo. "Jane's horses turned up and she's nowhere to be found. They're mighty scratched up and played out, so I think she's on foot somewhere in the Peace River hills."

"Whoa!" said Brian. "Slow down Jake. Slow down. What was Jane doing up in the hills? And when did the horses show up?"

"She was alone on a trail ride to Peace River through the hills," said Flo. "We seen the horses just a few minutes ago. We drove right in to tell you."

"Anything could have happened to her out there alone!" said Jake, exhausted. "It could have been bears! Or maybe she had an accident! What are you going to do? We need a search party and you can count me in…When're we leaving?"

Ray joined his boss at the counter and they asked Jake and Flo the usual 'missing persons' questions. But before they could take any notes, the detachment door banged open again and a soaking-wet woman and an equally wet dog flew inside.

"Morning, Marcy," said Ray. "The boss is busy, can I help you? Looks like you saw a ghost."

"Sam came to my place in the valley. You know, Jane's dog! This is him here, Sam. He had a can tied to his collar with a note inside. From Jane. She's down at the White Mud and the guys you're looking for are there. She's hiding out in the bush with the little kid, Devon, and an RCMP officer who's hurt real bad. Jane says those guys have guns! Here's the note."

Corporal Stevens took the still-damp note, read it and immediately called back Corporal Malone.

"Hey Lane...Brian Stevens again. We're going to need every body you've got. Looks like we found our missing policeman and that little kid everyone's been looking for."

Kip said, "I gotta take a leak, then we can eat."

Jane dropped down from her position below the window. If she could find out when they were leaving, she would chance leaving Mark and Devon and go for help. They'd be safe now, as long as they stayed put.

Suddenly there was a noise behind her and before she could react Kip had pushed the window open further and grabbed her hair, yanking her to her feet. Simon ran out the door proceeded to grab the fighting Jane around cabin and through the doorway, roughly pushing her towards the man shackled to the bed.

Simon said, "Well, well, well! What we got here? More company! Snooping around windows ain't real healthy-like, is it Kip?"

"Definitely not good for your health," agreed Kip. "Wonder how much she's heard?"

Jane was furious with herself for getting caught.

The two criminals gloated over their new prisoner. Simon reached over, and jerked Jane to the middle of the room where the light was better. "Okay bitch. What were you doing out there? Snooping around were you?"

"Hey, what the hell!" cried Jane with real anger. "Nothing! My car broke down about five miles back and I've been walking around looking for help. Lying through her teeth, she continued, "All I need is a phone. I saw your light and looked in the window to see if there was anyone home. Then I saw that one tied up on the floor...I got scared. Is that a *crime*? Who are you guys? And who's that guy?"

"Oh, he's a real bad criminal of sorts," chortled Kip. "The worst!"

"Yep," said Simon, "that's what he is. One of the worst you'll ever find. He's a baddie all right. Y'see, we're detectives and we followed and captured this guy. He's wanted in Edmonton. Easy as pie. He just sort of fell into our hands and here we are."

"Yeah, whatever. Looks like he's been giving you a bad time, but for cops you guys sure play rough," said Jane, trying to keep up her false front. "Look, I don't care what your business is with him. All I want is a phone. I need to get help for my car. I'm tired of walking. And if you don't have a phone, I'd sure like to shove off...Hey, you don't think I'm with him do you?

"Nope. And don't you worry, cause he ain't gonna trouble us much longer," said Simon with a chuckle. "And neither will you, 'cause you're staying right where you are. Y'see bitch, we ain't taking no chances, so you just sorta like park your ass on the floor near that desperado dude over there and we'll see what happens. Too bad we plumb run out of handcuffs. So you just sit real still like, and everybody'll be one big happy family. Got it?"

Jane shuffled over to Cam's corner and sat cross-legged on the floor.

"And no talking! And don't get any wise ideas. We're gonna eat...too bad there's not enough for you two," Simon said with a smirk.

Feeling helpless and scared, Jane eyed the distance to the door, watched the men go about fixing the meal, and cursed herself again for getting caught. She felt a repeating pressure against her back and looked around slowly to see Cam's pointing with motioning with his chin and staring at his feet.. Bewildered, Jane crinkled her eyebrows and again Cam motioned silently toward his feet. She suddenly caught on.

"Hey, guys," she said calmly, "do I have to sit like this or can I shift my position? You don't even have a rug down here."

"Do what you want, just don't try nothin' fancy or we might get excited."

When the men returned their attention to their meal, Jane moved her hands towards Cam's feet, running his hand under his shoe. Cam nodded his approval and she let her hand drift until it was near his pant cuff. There, she felt something hard. She recognized the shape of a key and an immense wave of relief swept over her.

Laughing, Simon slapped Kip on the back, "Good idea. Pretty close to what I was thinking." Still chuckling, Simon got up and went over to unlock Cam's shackled hands. "You're going for a nice little stroll with Kip." Cam knew what was coming. They were going to dispose of him, and do who knows what to the girl. It would not be quick, or painless. Walking stiffly, Cam shuffled through the door into the rain with Kip right behind him, gun at the ready.

Kip walked Cam to the edge of the clif, "Gotta have you in just the right place, pig. When you get to the bottom of the river say hello to one of your friends. He's waiting for you in his...uh...waterlogged...cop car."

"You son of a bitch," Cam said.

"Wasn't our fault," Kip joked, "...the stupid ass just drove right over the bank into the river. We really did want to save him, but we just couldn't."

Pointing the gun at Cam's chest, Kip said, "Any famous last words mister homicide officer boy?"

"None for you, you dirty bugger," Cam blurted as he pulled out the derringer that Jane had placed in his pocket only moments before. The bullet hit Kip square in the forehead. Kip's hand twitched with the impact shooting off a round into Cam's shoulder, knocking him down; Kip was dead before he hit the ground.

Inside the cabin Jane's horror was just beginning. A soon as Kip and Cam left, Simon said, as her dragged her up off the floor. He shoved Jane back until she felt the counter behind her. She felt around behind her, finding a heavy ceramic coffee pot. She grabbed it as he jerked her into his arms, pulling her by the hair and forcing her head back as far as it would go.

Her only option was to keep him distracted, keep him occupied. She pretended to relax and laughed, making out that she was enjoying herself.

Simon loosened his hold on her sneering, "Oh, a willing one. Well...it won't change the outcome bitch."

Taking advantage of his momentary weakness Jane screamed, smashing the coffee pot into his face with all her might. Simon staggered back and Jane pushed passed the stunned man, racing out the door into the rain. Heading to the riverbank, she saw two men on the ground. One was trying to get up and the other wasn't moving.

Running up to him, she saw the blood on Cam's shirt. "Hurry!" Jane said, pointing. "Run for those trees! The kid and Mark are in there in a brush pile ...about 500 yards... large broken spruce tree. Run!"

Just as Cam disappeared into the trees, Simon lurched out of the cabin, blood streaming down his face. Simon ran to check his brother and could see instantly that he was dead. He yelled after Jane, "Bitch! Now you're really going be sorry." He stopped for a moment and looked down at his dead brother, snarling, "You never could do nothin' right, could ya?"

Not seeing Cam, Simon looked into the water, satisfied that Kit had managed to push him into the river before he died. "Good!" he said, "Now I've just got that freaking bitch to deal with." Pulling Cam's service revolver from his belt, he started after Jane.

As she fled, Jane racked her brain for ideas. She had a jackknife and some wire in her pocket, there had to be some way to utilize them. Running full speed through the trees, she wondered how she could possibly fight him off, even in his weakened state. She knew she couldn't win on land, but if she could stay near the river...and if worse came to worse, she could jump over the cliff into the river and take her chances.

Simon's first shot whizzed past her and smacked into a tree beside her. Diving for cover, Jane crawled through the thick brush and spotted a coyote den under a dead tree. It was a tight fit, but with the help of the dead tree, she was able conceal enough of herself to be safe—she hoped.

Simon, rampaging through the bush like an angry moose, was close enough to the coyote den that Jane could hear him tearing back and forth. Even after the bush fell silent, she decided to wait until dark before backtracking and heading toward the Cadott. She hoped somebody might still be fishing. When darkness fell, she inched out of her hiding place into the dense trees. It was still raining and she was cold and hungry. But those things didn't matter because she knew she might still have to run for her life.

Cam staggered through the bush, spotted the dead spruce tree and found the brush pile. It wasn't much, but it was somewhat warm. At least it was out of the rain. He was wet and cold and knew he was losing a lot of blood. A little boy with big frightened eyes quietly stared up at him.

"Devon? Is that you?" Cam asked.

The little boy nodded, pointing at the man lying beside him and said, "Mark ... he's really sick...I keep him warm."

Cam spotted the first aid kit, "Could you help me Devon? I'm a policeman too and a bad guy shot me in the arm. Can you to help me put this cloth around my shoulder."

"Oh yes, I help my puppy all the time. He gets in trouble lots of times...Mommy and me put cloths bandaids on him." He started crying suddenly, "I want my mommy. I don't know why my daddy doesn't come." Cam scooped him up with his good arm and said, "Little buddy, your daddy can't come because he's hurt just like Mark. But we've got the whole world out looking for you."

Comforted and assured by Cam's kind manner, Devon helped him take off his shirt. Grimacing, the child said, "It's okay if you cry. It looks real bad."

Cam said, "If I cry, you won't tell on me, will you?"

Devon shook his head, solemnly. "I won't tell."

Looking around, Cam was relieved to see the rifle, shells, and an axe beside Mark. "Is Mark asleep?" asked Cam.

"Maybe," said Devon. "He's been real quiet for long time."

Cam shifted his way over to Mark and quickly assured the boy the officer was sleeping, and that he'd be alright.

"Devon, let's take the big gun and go find a nice warm cabin. Would you like that?"

Devon did not reply.

"It's warmer in a cabin," Cam added. "And you can have some soup."

"No," Devon said. "I wanna stay here. The bad mans hurt my arm."

"Devon, Mark can't stay here. He's too sick. When Mark is okay, you and me can get someone to help us." Cam knew his car keys were in Simon's pocket. "Devon, you have to help me carry the rifle. Get your shoes on and we can go."

"No shoes," Devon replied. "The bad mans took them."

"Well, little man, I'll just have to make two trips to the cabin. Want to come first? Just you, and we'll take the gun. Then I'll come back for Mark."

"Me first," Devon said, reaching for Cam's neck.

Groaning from the pain in his arm, Cam wiggled out of the shelter and called to Devon. "Okay, come out so I can carry you." He lifted the child and the rifle with his good arm, but Devon struggled to be put down. "I walk. You hurt real bad. Maybe you can't come back for Mark because you are crying."

"Okay, we can do that. But your feet are going to get cold." He set Devon down on the cold ground, threw the sleeping bag over the little boy's shoulders, and crawled back into the shelter for Mark. Hauling him out wasn't easy and it took everything Cam had to hoist the man's dead weight over his shoulder. Slumping over, he walked as quickly as he could, pausing every few seconds to catch his breath and to make sure Devon was behind him.

"Hey, Devon, you're doing a great job. Not much farther."

Devon was crying, scared, wet, and cold. "This is too heavy. I'm tired."

Cam panted, "Okay, okay. Just stay there and I'll come back for you as soon as I get Mark in the cabin."

The loss of blood had taken its toll on Cam, but he was determined to get Mark inside the cabin if it was the last thing he did. Stumbling through the open door, he dropped Mark's dead weight on the bed. Groaning, he fell to the floor, resting his head on the side of the bed. He couldn't have gone another step, he couldn't catch his breath, and he could feel the warmth of his blood trickling down his aching arm.

"Devon!" Cam called from inside the cabin. "Devon! Can you hear me? Where are you? Come in the cabin!"

The child did not appear. "Come on, Devon! I need your help."

With there was no response coming, Cam fought to get his body to its feet and staggered out the door. The little guy was standing at the edge of the trees, crying and shaking. Cam approached him and said, "The bad guys are not in here. Don't be afraid."

Cam leaned over, extending his good arm, and lifted the child. Devon wrapped his arms around Cam's neck and said, "The bad mans shot my daddy and made my mommy scream." Tears streamed down Cam's face. Some things were just too much. As they staggered toward the cabin, Devon said, "Your owie is real bad. I know it hurts. I fix it, don't cry."

"Kid, you've been gone for a long time and your daddy is in the Manning Hospital. And your mommy is going to be okay but she has to stay in the Edmonton hospital for a little while. When you get home, your dad will take you to see her."

Cam thought again of what this little boy seen and heard. He gently deposited Devon in a chair and checked the action and barrel of the rifle.

Cam fell into the easy chair, his eye to the door and his back facing away from windows. Despite his aching body, his mind was racing at full speed, trying to absorb the series of events that had shaken his life. He thought about the woman, a stranger, who was obviously nobody's fool. *She could have run the other way when she heard the gunfire. But she didn't, she ran toward me to see if I was okay.*

Wow, that's some dame, he almost said out loud.

Devon was asleep now and Mark's ragged breathing had slowed to a steady pace. Cam's thoughts turned back to Jane. She was now the only one Simon was after, and as far as she knew there was nobody around to help. She was offering her life for two men she didn't know and the little boy.

Would have been nice to have met her under different circumstances, Cam thought. *That would have been just fine, just mighty fine. A woman with brains, beauty, and guts.*

Cam doubted Simon would return to the cabin. But just to be sure, he locked the door and put the rifle on the table within easy reach.

He covered Mark with another quilt and put Devon in the bed beside him.

"Water. Water." Mark stared at Cam in puzzlement, "Who are you?"

"I'm RCMP, so you're okay," Cam said.

Anticipating the next question, Cam briefly explained the wild string of events had led him back here. "But just rest," Cam said. "We've got a gun here, the door is locked, and I doubt Drosset's coming' back. Here's some water, just a little bit now. I'm making soup. It's nearly ready."

"Man, I'm starved," groaned Mark.

"Me too!" said Devon, waking from his slumber

"Sure thing, buddy. I wasn't going to forget you. You can eat at the table with me soon as Mark has some."

When Mark finished, he breathed a quiet and satisfied, "good" and closed his eyes. Cam didn't know if he was sleeping or if he'd lapsed into unconsciousness again. Under the circumstances there wasn't much else he could do to help him either way.

Filling two more bowls, he sat at the table with Devon, who preferred to drink the soup. A spoon was far too slow. "Boy! You are some hungry," Cam said just as the door crashed open and a hollering team of RCMP filled the room.

Devon screamed and Cam hit the deck. Mark jerked awake, terrified that his nightmares were, in fact, a reality.

"Down! Down! Down!" yelled an officer. "Don't move! Don't move!" When the officers were sure the cabin was secure, they gave Cam a chance to speak. Devon had tentatively gone back to his soup.

"I'm Detective Cam Jensen, that's Constable Mark Snyder on the bed. I've been shot in the arm, Mark was slugged on the head...and this here is Devon, our missing boy." Cam heard somebody laugh at Devon's keen attention to his soup, breaking tension.

Corporal Lane Malone from the Peace River Detachment came into the cabin. "It was the Drosset brothers, wasn't it?" he asked. "Do you know where they are? You okay?"

"Yeah, I'm okay. One of them is dead," Cam said. "I shot him, but the other creep is after the woman who saved Mark, Devon, and me."

Lane exclaimed, "Which way did they go? We've got to get out there and help her."

"Yeah," said Cam. "The sooner we get going, the better..."

"Hey cool it," said Malone. "You aren't going anywhere with that shot-up arm. We got lots of guys here and we'll go after them. Just point the way and we'll leave someone here until an ambulance comes. I'm staying here, the rest of you guys get going."

Three times Simon had managed to get a lead on Jane and three times she managed to use the cover of the forest to elude him. She knew her luck wasn't going to last forever. She was scared to go to the bottom of the hill because away from the protection of the trees, he would easily spot her.

She climbed higher, staying along the cliffs. She had steeled herself to jump if it came to that. Creeping onto a bush-covered overhang, she looked over the edge and shuddered. It was a long way to the bottom.

Simon's cruel voice from behind her sent shivers up her spine, "Well, well, well. Nowheres to run now bitch." Spinning around she couldn't believe the killer had caught up with her.

Simon moved in on her, "Well this is just perfect, ain't it? I don't even have to waste a bullet, sweetie. You can just fall off the edge and hope you hit a cliff on your way down. That would be nice and quick, and easy...and saves me making all that noise. Pretty convenient."

Jane knew he was right. To clear the cliff face, she needed a running jump. She should have done it when she'd had the chance, but now it was too late.

Suddenly, Jane drew in a sharp intake of breath. Simon puzzled at her widening eyes.

Jane couldn't believe it; coming up quickly and quietly behind Simon was a cinnamon-coloured bear—a bear with one ear.

Jane grinned and said softly, "There's a bear behind you."

"Try again," Simon snarled, "I'm not gonna fall for some dumb-ass oldie like that. You ready for a nice little flying lesson?" No sooner had he spoken those words than he felt hot breath on his neck and the drip of saliva on his head.

Whirling around, his hand flashed to his gun, but the bear batted quickly it away.

The animal dropped to its feet, throwing its head from side to side, its eyes fixed on Simon. Simon grabbed Jane and threw her in front of the bear. Falling at the bear's feet, Jane noticed the back leg had no fur around it—there was no question it was Baldie! The bear roughly rolled her over, sniffed her, and then rolled her out of the way, turning its attention to the man who was now trying to scramble around him. But the bear was enormous and easily blocked any escape to the forest.

The bear clubbed Simon down, clawing and mauling him. Glancing over the cliff, Simon knew he had to jump. He knew he was dead either way—the bear, the cliff face, or the water—it didn't matter. Ultimately the bear took the choice away from him. Shaking him back and forth like a rag doll, the bear flung Simon over the cliff.

Not waiting to see the outcome, Jane had already torn off running into the forest. She paused only briefly for a moment to recognize the deadly silence following the man's screams of sheer terror.

Cam and Corporal Taylor were sitting on the cabin porch, discussing their options, when a car spun into the driveway and slammed on its brakes. Lane's hand automatically dropped to his gun, but relaxed when Marcy and Sam jumped out.

"Marcy! What are you doing here?" Corporal Taylor inquired.

"I brought Sam. If Jane's out there with that madman, Sam can track her for you."

Cam groaned as he pulled on a shoulder holster but Stevens stopped him, "Cam, you better stay here. You're in lousy shape."

"Not this time. I have to go. She risked her life for all of us and I have to help if I can."

⸹

Jane saw the bear ambling toward her. *Now what?*

Just then she could hear a dog barking in the distance. It was a very familiar bark. Sam! She'd know that bark anywhere. He peeked his head through the brush and behind him was a string of six police officers and the detective from the cabin. Jane hollered at them to stay where they were and to hold Sam back.

The officers watched intently with guns drawn as the bear closed in on her. It sniffed the air and growled, waving its head from side to side.

"Easy Baldie...easy Baldie," Jane said, her heart in her throat. "No one's going to hurt you." The bear relaxed at the sound of Jane's voice and her gentle tone. He came closer. Then, stopping just inches from her, he stuck out his tongue and licked her face. Jane tentatively reached out and petted the animal's huge head.

"Okay bear. You've got to get going before somebody gets trigger-happy. If Sam gets loose, he'll try to tear you apart, so go on. Beat it. We're even. Have a happy life and stay away from hunters."

The bear turned around and disappeared into the thick pine and spruce trees. Jane waved to the officers to let Sam go. He bounded up and knocked her over with joy. As the officers reached her, Jane's strength and reserve crumbled and she started to cry.

"I'm *so* glad to see you guys. I couldn't stand to see anyone else hurt."

Cam gave her a one-armed hug, "Thank you so much! None of us would be alive right now if it hadn't been for you."

An officer ran back down to the cars to radio in to get a patrol boat to check for Simon's body downstream.

"Come on, you two," Lane said. "There's an ambulance coming to get Mark out. We'll get you checked over real good in town. It's about 12 miles back to the cabin...think you can make it Cam?"

"Don't know how I feel," Cam said. "Kind of queasy. But I'll try. Jane could help me I guess."

"Whatever," laughed Jane. " I think it's your turn to help me for a change."

Cam looked at Jane, "What you did back there was damn brave of you."

"Brave is an understatement," said Lane. "But we want to know why that big bear didn't attack. It seemed like you knew each other."

"Seems I'm in the habit of saving bears," Jane explained. "I'm just glad that he didn't pick *me* to throw over the cliff."

As they trudged back to the cabin, Jane explained how she'd lost her horses and ended up on foot in the middle of nowhere. "My bear was a lot more friendly than the grizzly that ran my horses off."

"What grizzly?" Brian asked.

"The one that's dead back on the trail where I had to leave all my gear. So if you're going that way to search for Drosset's body, will you get someone to pick up all my stuff?"

"Jane, it couldn't be a grizzly," said Lane. "We don't have them around here. You know that."

"Lane, when you get my stuff, take a good look. That's exactly what I told myself when he was standing over of me and I was rolling around on the ground trying to get a shot off. He knew he was a grizzly. And I knew he was trouble." Everyone laughed and Cam couldn't help but appreciate her sense of humour.

Once they'd made their way back to the cabin an officer relayed the message from the boat patrol, "Corporal Malone, the patrol called in. Says they can't find that guy's body."

Lane replied, "Not surprised. The current probably washed it further downstream or maybe it's hooked on something underwater. Keep in touch with the boat guys, okay? And let me know if they find anything."

Turning to two of the officers, he said, "Torbett and McCready, you guys go back to where Jane left her stuff on the trail. Ask her for directions. And keep your eyes open for a dead grizzly...yeah...a grizzly."

Despite his continued blood loss, Cam remained captivated by Jane as they drove into town in the ambulance. His heart seemed to jump in his chest when she spoke to him. He avoided looking into her eyes and tried to keep himself from gazing at her. She was beautiful, even though she was an absolute mess.

As for Jane, her mind was going a mile a minute. When Jane's eyes met Cam's, she too found herself floundering for words. Her throat kept tightening and she felt like a tongue-tied teenager. There was something about him that drew her emotions to the surface. She'd never had such a visceral reaction to a man. She'd had her share of broken relationships, and she had become leery of men. She'd long ago given up on trying to meet society's expectations that she just settle down with whatever man that would take her. But suddenly, right in front of her might the man she had been looking for all of her life. Trouble was—he didn't know it.

They took Cam into the hospital's emergency ward as soon as they arrived at the hospital. The swelling in Mark's brain was increasing, and he was taken to surgery immediately. His wife Andi met the ambulance and she stopped to tearfully thank Jane.

Cam too was in need of surgery to remove the bullet lodged in his shoulder and he was whisked off to an operating room. Corporal Stevens sat with Jane in the waiting room. "Do you

"Let's go now and then I'll go home for a shower and a sleep."

They made their way back to the station, where all the officers that had been called in to deal with the case gathered around to listen. The men became very quiet as she told them how Mark had been attacked, stuffed into his car, and shoved over the cliff into the river.

Jane wasn't the only one to become emotional as she recounted the harrowing experience of trying to pull him out of the sinking car. By the time she'd finished her state-ment, Jane found herself shaken and exhausted—in dire need of sleep.

Jane bid the officers goodbye and told them she would be back in a couple of hours. Corporal Stevens walked her to a cruiser and helped her in, "Ray's taking you home. I'm going back to the hospital to check on Cam and I'll phone you in a couple hours. That'll give you some down time."

"Thanks, Brian," she said. "I'll expect your call."

Brian nodded, "You go rest and I'll see you later."

Brian hadn't been waiting long when Dr. Adams came down the hallway, clapping his hands. "Good news, Brian! We got the bullet out okay. He's lost a lot of blood, but otherwise he'll be fine. With lots of R and R, he'll be good as new. In a few days, he can go home if he has someone to look after him."

Brian called Jane within the hour to tell her the good news and that evening Jane she made her way back to the hospital. She found Stevens still visiting with Cam. "Hey," she said as she came into the room. "You still in bed?"

"Hey yourself," replied Cam. "Glad to see you back. Didn't think you'd come tonight."

"Had to be here," she grinned. "Had to make sure you didn't croak or something. And I had to see how that hand-some police officer was doing."

Stevens laughed and poked Cam. He had already noticed that the rugged man in the bed was smitten with his rescuer. "We were just discussing where Cam gonna stay when he's discharged from hospital," explained Stevens. "Maybe we should just ship him back to Ottawa and be done with it. What do you think Jane? Or I could take him to our place and put him in the basement. With four kids, two dogs, and a cat, having him around won't make much difference."

They laughed. "You're such a comedian, Brian," Jane smiled. "But I have an extra room and he can stay at the farm until he makes other arrangements." *I must be nuts,* Jane thought. *Why can't I keep my big mouth shut?* But she could hardly keep her eyes off Cam. *How in the world will I handle being close to him night and day?*

But before she could take the idea any further, Cam gave her a reprieve, "I'll take your offer, Brian. The basement sounds good enough for me." He looked at Jane and gave her a smile that could melt an igloo and said, "But thanks for the offer, Jane."

Cam did his best not to betray his thoughts. *How in the world would I be able to stay with her and manage to keep my hands off her?* Since the moment he'd first laid eyes on her, all he wanted to do was hold her. As she spoke, he watched her lips and she caught a flash of desire in his eyes. She quickly looked away. A thrill ran through her — a thrill unlike any she had ever known. This man had taken her heart.

She shrugged to indicate she didn't care that he had turned down her invitation. *I live a quiet life and don't need some guy messing up my tranquillity,* she told herself as she bade him good night. But she couldn't had to admit she felt more than a twinge of disappointment in her heart. Looking back at Brian, she said, "Call me if you need help, you know, reports and stuff." It was lame and she knew it, but it would have to do in her effort to ignore Cam.

Two days later Cam phoned, asking directions to where she lived.

"Sure, but why?" Jane asked.

"Well," he said, "is that offer still open to stay out at your place?"

"Well, yeah, I guess so," she replied. "What's up?"

"It's bedlam at Brian's place. Four screaming kids bouncing all over me. The dogs like to play tag with me. The kids chase the dogs, the dogs go crazy when the rabbit escapes or when they're after the cat. Toys everywhere."

Laughing, she said, "Give my best to Brian and come on out." Tidying up a bit, she hurried into her bedroom and slipped on a white sundress. In the kitchen, she got a out bottle of rye and a couple of cans of Pepsi and set them out on the veranda table. Going back in, she dug some ice cubes out of the icebox and had just fixed a drink when he drove into the yard. Setting her drink down, she walked out into the sunlight to meet him.

"Hey, Cam. How'd you get here so fast? It's 20 miles to Manning and you're here already!"

Cam grinned, "I broke a few traffic laws, it helps having a badge."

Jane laughed at his boldness, "I've never seen a guy with your kind of nerve!"

"Yeah, I guess," shrugged Cam ruefully. "And I've never met a woman with your kind of class!"

Laughing, she helped him out of the car, realizing for the first time what a big man he was. Putting her arm around his waist to steady him, she said, "My goodness, it's the jolly green giant. I feel like a kernel of corn beside you. I didn't realize how tall you were."

"I've been called a lot of things, but never the jolly green giant," Cam laughed.

Helping him to a veranda chair, she ran back to his car for his bag. He watched her closely, admiring how gracefully she moved. She was beautiful and he couldn't believe she hadn't yet married. As Jane put the bag in the spare bedroom, she thought how nice it would be to have some company for a change, especially this kind of company.

She went back to the veranda and settled into a chair beside him. They passed the afternoon getting to know each other better. He told her about his life in Ontario and how he'd gotten involved in the Simon Drosset case. They broke into fits of laughter as he explained how he had managed to survive two days at the Stevens home with four kids, two dogs, a cat, and a rabbit. After a light supper they talked their way late into the night. Finally, at two in the morning, Jane said, "You're supposed to get your rest and we've talked half the night."

Showing him to his room and setting out some fresh towels for him, she said goodnight. She thought she would lie in bed for the rest of the night thinking about him, but sleep overtook her as soon as her head touched the pillow.

The next few days passed quickly. Jane couldn't remember when life had seemed so smooth and wonderful. Hands touching accidentally, eyes meeting, sharing jokes, going for walks together, playing with Sam, tending to the still-recovering horses—she had never felt so alive. And despite her best intentions to keep things above the board, the inevitable did happen.

One morning she met Cam in the hallway, as he'd emerged from the shower, wearing only his panama bottoms and tousling dry his damp hair. Looking into Jane's still-sleepy eyes, he melted. He had never seen anyone so sensual and beautiful. Reaching out, he used his good arm and pulled her gently to him. He kissed her deeply; there was no stopping now. Jane was pulled in. *Nature can just take its course*, she thought, clinging to him and blissfully drowning in his kisses.

Cam couldn't believe how he felt about this woman. He marvelled at how quickly a person could fall in love. There was no question in his mind that his next step would be to set up a transfer from Ottawa to Alberta.

After being enthralled with his company for two weeks, Jane woke one morning to find him dressed and his bag packed. With her heart beating so hard she could hear it in her ears, she said as calmly as she could, "You leaving?"

"Yeah. Got deadlines to meet and unfinished business to put in order. I've been gone a long time and they need me in Ottawa." He leaned over and kissed her cheek, "Take care. I'll be in touch."

She was speechless. What was that supposed to mean? Dumbfounded, her legs trembling, she watched him climb into his car. Waving once more, he drove out of the yard and—she was convinced—out of her life.

Falling to her knees, she held her face in her hands and cried her heart out. How could he just walk out after all the tender words he'd uttered, after the intimacy and passion they'd shared? And to end it with four little word, *I'll be in touch*.

Wham! Bam! Thank you ma'am. She felt used. Discarded. Humiliated.

A month went by and Jane kept to herself, nursing her badly bruised heart. Each day she waited close to the phone for a call and each day she lost a little more hope. He could at least have had the decency to give her a call. Hearing the news that Mark had made it home safely to his family and that Devon had been reunited with his parents only cheered her heart slightly. It seemed everyone was enjoying a happy ending—everyone but her, that is.

How long Simon had lay there on the sandbar more dead than alive he did not know.

But when his mind had cleared, he had pulled his broken body further inland towards a cabin in the distance. As he crawled toward it he vowed that if he made it through this, he would settle a few scores.

The last thirty yards to the cabin door all but did Simon in. After resting to catch his breath he pulled himself up, turned the doorknob, and pushed it open. He crawled through the doorway over to the bunk bed, pulled off a blanket and wrapped it around his shivering body, collapsing on the bed. He fell asleep instantly, waking some time later as wracking pain coursed through his body. He had no idea how long he'd been there—couldn't tell if it was hours or days. Using the bunk for leverage he pulled himself to his feet, cursing the pain. He looked around and spotted a half-full pail of water sitting on an old washstand.

He groaned as he pulled off his wet clothes and realized that he'd cracked more than a few ribs as he bounced over and over against the cliff wall before hitting the water. The bear had squeezed the living hell out of him and its claw marks were deep and still bleeding. Where the animal had bitten into his shoulder his skin hung in shreds; an entire huge chunk of flesh had been ripped away from the bone. At the sight of it, Simon threw up all over himself and collapsed onto a heap on the floor.

He spotted some towels beneath the washstand and crawled over to them. He lay there for some time, and then with the little strength he had left he ripped them into strips and washed his wounds as best as he could. After a few more minutes rest he covered them with the makeshift bandages.

He realized that he was getting weaker by the second and that if he didn't get something to eat soon he'd be in real trouble. Dragging himself over to the small cupboard, steadying himself against the all. He found some cans of stew and an opener and wolfed down their contents. Then he groped his way back to the bunk He barely had the strength to grab the blanket from the floor, groaning with pain as he pulled it up and over him. Just before he passed out rage overtook him and he snarled through his teeth. "I'm coming for you woman...even if it's the last thing I do in this life."

After 12 days or so of sleeping and moving only in order to eat or relieving himself Simon decided he was going to make it through. As he grew stronger he knew he had to figure a way to get himself up the steep cliffs and find his way back to civilization.

So he packed the remaining food in a blanket and started the trek up the cliff. His body still weak, the climb quickly became a true endurance test. His hatred for that woman was his driving force, and his rage knew no bounds. It was her fault that Kip was dead and it was her fault the bear had mauled him. Everything that had happened seemed to involve the bitch. And no woman had ever bested him and lived to tell the story.

After a nerve-wracking struggle he managed to climb up the cliff but had no idea where he was. When the food ran out he ate berries, and even uprooted rotten logs to get at the grub worms, ants, and spiders. He thought he was making progress, but he'd been walking in circles for days and eventually found himself back where he'd started. Cursing vehemently, he started all over again. But still, his frenzied hatred for that woman drove him on.

All day the hot sun beat down unmercifully upon him. With no water his lips blistered and his throat ached. He didn't think it could possibly get worse. But it always did. Night came and with it horse flies, sand flies, and mosquitoes. They all but ate him alive. He was delirious and near-crazed from it all.

He eventually came across a nearby slew and crawled on hands and knees into the rank, dead water. It was so foul –smelling even the bugs were avoiding it. He drank his fill then lay there for some time to ease the swelling and itching from insect bites. Any movement he made caused the slime and mud from the bottom of the slough to turn the water murky around him. As he lay, there trying not to gag from the smell, he heard the whinnying of a horse. Rolling his body onto his belly he carefully parted the tall slough grass.

To his utter amazement atop the horse sat that despised woman.

His first instinct was to chase her down and wrench her from the horse's back. But common sense and the throbbing pain in his body soon quelled his instincts. He knew there was no way he could overtake the horse in his condition. He decided the best tactic was to follow her and take her by surprise. As she turned the horse to leave, a huge Collie appeared barking and growling. It was headed straight for the slough and Simon. Grabbing a reed he broke it off, put it in his mouth, and pushed himself back into the deeper part of the slough and ducked under the water.

Sam stood by the slough, thoroughly confused. He was sure he had smelt something unusual and had seen it move. But when he heard Jane call to him, he turned around and trotted back to his mistress.

Cam arrived back in Alberta with a heavily-loaded and recently acquired pickup truck. He was on his way back to the woman he loved. In his pocket was the biggest sparkler he could afford and as he drove, he rehearsed his proposal.

He felt bad that he hadn't called her in his absence, but with all the work he'd had to do at work—catching up, tying up loose ends—he'd just been so swamped. But she knew how he felt, didn't she? He'd started to feel a bit edgy about it all. *I should have made sure she feels the same way I so. Maybe she doesn't. Maybe it was just a fling for her. I should have phoned. Why didn't I phone? Shit, it's been six weeks. Time enough for her to have second thoughts about all this.*

It never crossed his mind that she felt used and betrayed. It had never entered his head to phone and explain that he'd gone back to end his story in Ontario and start a new chapter with her.

That evening Jane was feeling particularly down. For some inexplicable reason she felt uneasy as the afternoon drifted into evening. She was restless and had trouble settling down to do anything. Just as it was getting dark, she heard Sam barking hysterically, followed suddenly by dead silence.

"Sam where the hell are you? I wish you'd get your dumb ass home where it belongs!" she exclaimed out loud to herself.

A few minutes later, she opened the door and called for him again. Hearing nothing, she started to close the door to hear a voice whisper, "Sam's not available. Will I do?"

Simon Drosset pushed his foot into the doorway as she screamed and tried to slam the door shut. How could he be alive? She'd seen what the bear had done. She'd seen him fly over the cliff's edge and out of sight. It never occurred to her or anyone else that not finding the body could mean he was still alive.

Propelled by his push, she flew across the room and slammed into the table. The look in his eyes told her he was intent on killing her. And there would be nobody to save her this time. No dog. No bear.

He was hideous. He looked like the walking dead with open running sores, red, inflamed slashes across his face, torn clothing, and a crazed look unmatched by even the most enraged wild animal.

"And you thought between you and that damn bear you got rid of me, didn't you?" he sneered. "Sit on the couch, bitch, while I figure out what I'm gonna to do to you."

He went over to the fridge, pulled out some bread, baloney, and milk. The food disappeared quickly and he poured the milk in his open mouth, most of it running down his chin onto his shredded filthy clothing.

Jane's brain was screaming, she had no idea how she was going to get out of this.

When Drosset was distracted for just a moment, she grabbed a stainless steel letter opener from the coffee table and managed to work it up her sleeve out of sight just before her tormentor came back. He grabbed her by the shoulders and jerked her to her feet, saying, "C'mon how about a little fun, a reward. You want it bitch...I know your type..."

Suddenly Jane pulled back and raised her arms over her head in one swift smooth motion. Simon lost his balance and staggered back a step or two. Jane swung her arms down with all her strength and stabbed Simon with the letter opener. It wasn't until the burst of blood hit her that she realized she'd hit him in the eye.

Falling to his knees, he roared with pain, trying to brush away the blood. But it just kept coming. Jane ran through the still-open door into the night.

"Sam! Sam!" she yelled. "Sam. Where are you? Sam!" Running toward the corral, she rolled under the fence, driven by Drosset's crazed and threatening bellows.

Past the corral and barn, she saw the bale stack and shoved herself into a small space opening beside, pulling another bale in front of her as camouflage. Simon was staggering around, but getting closer. The sound of her heart in her head felt almost as loud as his roars. Jane tried to hold her breath, terrified the dust would cause her to cough or sneeze.

She knew that if he found her, he would kill her. He'd kill her the second he got his hands on her.

As Cam drove through the darkness, his headlights picked up something writhing on the road. Slamming on the brakes, he jumped out of his truck to find Sam badly beaten and stabbed. He was all but dead. Cam's heart rate kicked into high gear. There was something seriously wrong here. He carefully picked up the big dog, whispering encouraging words, and gently put him in the back of the pickup. Parking the truck on the side of the road road, he turned out the lights. Sam emitted a small whine.

"Take it easy, Sam, Jane's first. Hang in there."

He looked towards the house and saw the lights shining through the open door. His practised eye took in the spilled milk, the spray of fresh blood on the floor, and signs of a struggle in the living room. The next second he heard a bloodcurdling scream from beyond the corral.

Simon had grabbed Jane by the hair and pulled her out from behind the bales of hay. "You shouldn't leave the end of your nice white shirt showing, you dumb bitch. So *nice* to meet you again." Grabbing her neck, he began to squeeze. Hard. She struggled to break his powerful grip, kicking and clawing at him with her tied hands. As blackness overtook her, she heard a gunshot.

Running towards the hay stack, Cam saw a man bending Jane backwards, squeezing the life out of her. Cam fired his pistol and the shot jerked the assailant around. A stunned Simon Drosset fell to the ground. Pushing past him to get to Jane, Cam let his gun fall to the ground.

Putting his gun back into its holster, Cam ran over to Jane and pulled her into his arms as he knelt beside her. She was breathing, but only just. As he untied her hands she opened her eyes and looked past him. She started screaming, but it was too late. Something hit him hard on the back of his head. Falling forward on top of Jane, he tried rolling to one side as he groped for his gun.

Dazed and disoriented, Cam was struggling to get to his feet when he heard the shot. Jane had grabbed his gun and had used its last bullet. Screaming, she scrambled backward as Simon Drosset fell once more to the ground. This time there was no movement; the bullet had hit him between the eyes.

Jane scrambled on her hands and knees as fast as she could into Cam's arms. As they both lay breathless and spent on the ground, he wrapped his arms around her and held her tight, "Everything's going to be okay."

Cam gently coaxed Jane her to her feet. "Come on Jane, we've got to get back to my pickup. Sam's in the back and he's been hurt."

Barely able to walk, Jane gasped, "What happened... heard him...barking...then nothing."

Cam helped her to the truck and half-lifted, half-rolled her into the back of the pickup and onto a pile of blankets with Sam. He slowly turned the vehicle around and headed for town and a vet.

"Doesn't look good, Jane," the vet told her. "The stab wounds are deep and he took a hell of a beating. We've tried everything, Jane. All I can do now is give him enough medicine to dull the pain. His vital signs aren't good, so don't hold your breath."

Jane petted Sam sorrowfully. Deep in her heart she knew he wouldn't make it. After a half-hour, Sam took a final ragged breath and Jane laid her head against him and wept.

Cam watched as her heart broke. He felt defeated. There was nothing he could do to comfort her. That brave dog had saved all of their lives. Cam walked over to the phone to let Marcy know that Jane needed a friend who would understand her broken heart.

While they waited for Marcy, Cam detected a distinct chill from Jane. He told Jane he had called Marcy. She nodded blankly at him and turned to the vet to make arrangements to have Sam cremated. She then sat quietly with her hands folded in her lap, staring straight ahead.

Before Marcy and Jane left for the night, Cam said he'd go out to her place to check on everything. Jane nodded absently and said, "Yeah, sure. Thanks, I guess."

He knew she was grief-stricken, but it seemed like something else was wrong, and he didn't know what. Was it because he couldn't save Sam? Had he misjudged her feelings for him after all?

The police were just leaving as Cam arrived at Jane's farm. He talked to Corporal Stevens for a while and decided to park his truck in town—he felt uneasy leaving it in Jane's yard. He had expected her to welcome him with open arms, especially given the situation. Jane had been clearly uncomfortable with him being at the vet's and couldn't wait to get away. She hadn't even said goodbye when she left with Marcy. But by the time he reached town C was exhausted. He needed a good night's sleep. He'd be able think more clearly in the morning.

Cam was sullenly drinking down a coffee in the motel restaurant when Stevens came by.

"Morning, Brian," Cam said, glumly. "Join me for toast? I'm buying."

"Sure, sounds good."

As they waited for their order Brian asked, "So, how're you doing today?"

Cam's non-committal grunt and intent focus on Manning's empty main street gave Brian the lead he wanted. "The shooting bothering you, Cam?"

"No...it's Jane. Here I was...put my house on the market in Ottawa, resigned from a good job, drove all the way out here...couldn't wait to see her. And she totally cold-shouldered me. I mean...I know she is really heartbroken about losing Sam. But she's distanced herself from me. She's really icy. Everything I own is in that frigging truck. And I've got a ring burning a hole in my pocket."

Brian thanked the waiter for the toast and ordered a coffee, "You want the straight goods or a snow job?"

Cam raised an eyebrow, "Shoot!"

"Cam, you better have a good long talk with Jane. When you left here, you told no one you were coming back. You were gone weeks and never once called Jane, as far as I know. I'd see her now and then, and ask if she'd heard from you yet. But I quit asking after she burst into tears one day and told me never to mention your name again. Said it hurt too much. What the hell's with that? I could tell she was thoroughly humiliated."

Cam shifted uncomfortably, checked Main Street again, and started to say something, thought better of it, and continued to ignore his coffee.

"I don't know what you told Jane when you left, but I don't think it was much. She told me you said you'd be in touch. You never told her you were selling anything or changing jobs or moving here. Nothing! I think as far as Jane was concerned, you had a nice two-week fling, thanked her for the good time, and buggered off. I felt so sorry for her I promised myself that if I ever saw you again, I was going to pop you one and tell you it was from Jane."

Cam was stunned. He suddenly sat up straight and froze—just as a deer in caught in headlights. He was horrified when it dawned on him that Brian was right. It was true: he hadn't said a word to Jane. He had figured they both felt the same way and that she knew what he was planning. He had told her he liked this part of the country and that he wouldn't mind living here, and he made the assumption that Jane would see this as a commitment. He'd never been good with words. And for God's sake, he thought she knew how he felt and besides, he'd wanted to surprise her with the ring.

But why hadn't he called? What was the real reason? It wasn't as though he hadn't thought about it, he'd wanted to...but he had stopped himself each time. Now it all came to him in a rush. He hadn't called because in the back of his mind he wondered if it might be possible that for her, it had just been a fling—and that terrified him.

"Damn it," he said, his voice little more than a whisper ... "How am I *ever* going to dig myself out of this mess?"

Brian just sat there and shrugged, "Beats me."

Jane awoke to hear Marcy banging around downstairs. Slipping out of bed, she made her way to the kitchen.

"Feeling better?" Marcy said as she hugged her.

"No," Jane said. "I feel like I was run over by a truck. Drosset's gone and that's good. Sam's gone and that's bad. And *he's* back from Ottawa. Walks in bold as brass. How could he do this to me? What kind of person does that?"

"Jane, Jane, Jane. You are trying to process too much at one time. Eat something and you'll feel better."

"I'm not hungry. All I want right now is a shower and a long walk."

"Phooey on that—you need to talk. Talk to me!" demanded Marcy. Jane finally broke down and recounted the night's harrowing events.

"And then, out of the blue, there's big ole Cam, saving my life! I thank God he was there at the right time. But he didn't even phone me. Not once. Not even a note in the mail. What am I supposed to think? I haven't heard a thing from him since he left. What kind of jerk does that?"

"He used me, he had his fun, and he left me. I hate him. I just hate him. I don't know why he came back or why he turned up last night. Maybe he got fired and needs a place to stay. Or maybe he came back on vacation, for a few quickies..."

She stopped to catch her breath. Marcy handed her a Kleenex, as Jane's shoulders began to shake and she sobbed into her hands.

"Well, if you really want to know how he feels about you I'd say just ask him... he just drove into the yard."

Jane jumped up. "Oh shit! Pyjamas! I'm still in pyjamas! How am I going to let him have it like this...I'm a mess," she sobbed.

"Yep," grinned Marcy, "and your hair looks like hell and you've got no time for makeup. You got about 10 seconds to get those tears off your face, girl."

Stunned, Jane froze on the spot as Marcy greeted him at the door.

"Morning, Marcy. Jane up yet?"

Marcy, with a wide smile, nodded as Jane walked past her and stepped onto the veranda. Looking him straight in the eye she said, "And what do *you* want?" Last night she'd been too weak and dazed to say what was on her mind. But at this moment she was determined she could handle anything.

Cam, taken aback by her reaction, swallowed hard and said, "Jane...please...please let me explain. I made plans to move out here, to quit my job in Ontario, to get a job in Alberta. I was so worried that might tell me not to come. Okay...was a fool. I was only thinking of myself. I was crazy not to make it clear to you what I was doing, what I wanted. I'm no damn good with words. I thought you knew how I felt. What an ass I've been."

Marcy moved away from the door, cleared the table, and made some more coffee. Jane, not sure if she should stand or run, kept looking up into the tall, quivering man's eyes.

"I just figured," Cam said, "that you knew I loved you and that I was coming back."

Silence.

Then, sobbing and with a touch of sarcasm, Jane said, "Oh yeah, of course I figured that after you didn't bother to get in touch even once over almost two months. Not a word from you! What did you expect me to think?"

Jane softened, "I didn't know what to think, because you somehow also forgot to tell me how you felt."

Cam looked into her dark, angry eyes and said, "Jane, I'm telling you now. I love you. I'm sorry about how I handled everything. I blew it and I need you to forgive me."

He pulled out the little box and opened it up to reveal the ring inside. "But this is how certain I was about us. The matching band is in the truck."

Watching him stumble and fumble through his proposal, Jane's heart lurched. Then, slowly, she felt her anger and resentment dissipate. Still, she didn't know what to believe or how to think.

Cam was kept talking, something about a pick-up truck, and something bout being really sorry that he'd taken so much for granted. But Jane didn't hear much of anything he said.

"So you had the ring in the pick-up?" Jane asked, trying to slip back into some form of reality, before realizing that she wasn't making sense.

She took a half-step towards Cam, as if being closer to him would bring her out of her daze.

"No, I had the ring in my pocket. Now you're getting me all confused," said Cam, shaking his head.

"Oh," mumbled Jane, stepping toward him.

"Well," Cam said, putting both her hands into one of his and reaching into his pocket. "Nothing seems to have made sense between us since I left. Let's see if the ring does." He flicked open the box, took out the ring, and placed it on her finger.

She stared at it silently before quietly saying, "It's a perfect fit," and walked into his waiting arms.

ABOUT BEVERLY LEIN

Beverly Lein was born in Canada, in the northern town of Manning, and grew up in nearby Sunny Valley on her father's farm near the mighty Peace River.

Beverly's many jobs consisted of running her own confectionary, clerking, managing the Shell bulk station along with her husband Carson, grain farming and farming elk.

Farming elk prompted Bev's first book *An Elk In The House*, published in 2006 by Newest press in Edmonton.

A true story that has one laughing one minute and crying the next.

Her next book *The Three Saints Of Christmas* was published in 2009 By Inkwater Press from Portland, Oregon. It is a must read for all readers of all ages that believe in miracles, saints, angels, and Santa Claus. In this adventurous and compelling fictional story it takes Santa, Gabriel and St. Joseph to get a family all together for Christmas in 1866.

To the Saint's credit they do well, but to their surprise they find looking after five children a bigger job than they could ever have imagined.

Her third book *Wolf Spirit The Story of Moon Beam* was published in 2010, again by Inkwater Press from Portland Oregon.

This fictional adventure is about a ten year old girl's struggle for survival. A pack of wolves, and her loyal black horse accompany her in this struggle.

She finds love with an Indian chief, but they clash because of their cultural differences.

This book is a must for anyone who likes fast-paced drama, wildlife and romance.

As a mother of two and grandmother of five, Bev honed her natural-born storyteller's instinct on those around her.

She still spends many late nights and pre-dawn mornings writing her thoughts, fantasies, and story lines.

Her grandchildren are her sounding board and her avid critics, but most of all her greatest fans.

Bev's wild and adventurous stories are timeless, and they appeal to young and old.

What makes Beverly, her editor, and other professionals around her, especially Inkwater Press, confident that her book are relevant to you her readers?

IN HER OWN WORDS:

I have been a avid reader of fiction since I was eight years old.

With no electric lights in our remote farmhouse, books were read in semi-darkness or with a flashlight. My mother insisted that I was going to go blind reading in the dark.

When my tasks were left undone my books were taken away from me. As a child who was sometimes deprived of books for various reasons, I created my own stories in my head and continue to do so in writing today.

I love being off on an exciting adventure in my own little world.

I am still at my age amazed that I can still pick up a book and get hopelessly caught up in it.

Whenever I buy a new book I turn back into that kid again and I am just as excited as I was back then.

My biggest dream is to share these feelings of wonderment and adventures with all of you.

BEV

CPSIA information can be obtained at www.ICGtesting.com
Printed in the USA
LVOW110026010512

279749LV00005B/1/P